POWDER
for
BUNKER HILL

POWDER

for

BUNKER HILL

Robert P. Richmond

Macrae Smith Company

Philadelphia

Library of Congress Catalog Card Number 68-31143
MANUFACTURED IN THE UNITED STATES OF AMERICA

6609

POWDER
for
BUNKER HILL

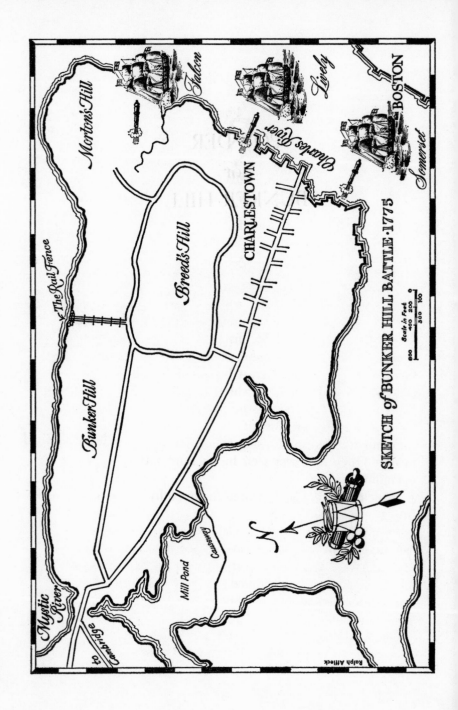

SKETCH of BUNKER HILL BATTLE · 1775

Scale in Feet

Mystic River

to Cambridge

Bunker Hill

Morton's Hill

The Rail Fence

Breed's Hill

CHARLESTOWN

Mill Pond

Causeway

Charles River

Falcon

Lively

Somerset

BOSTON

Ralph Affleck

I

Warm laughter filled the room. It surrounded Caleb, washed over him, eddied about him. Gasping laughter of Gramps, as he choked on his pipe smoke, laughed and wheezed, and choked again. Deep-throated laughter of Gram Page, jiggling her great bulk, shaking the wide, specially constructed chair in which she sat. And his father, Caleb noted with wonder—he too was laughing. At least, Caleb was willing to identify as laughter a series of harrumphings and grunts issuing from John Stark. It was the nearest Caleb had ever seen his taciturn father approach open mirth.

Watching him, Caleb winced in sympathy as his father's display of pleasure ended in a muttered oath. A sudden twist as John Stark turned to Caleb's mother, seated alongside him on the sofa, must have pained his sprained ankle. Molly Stark placed a comforting hand on her husband's arm as he glared at the injured member, wrapped in bandages covering ankle and foot, that was propped on a footstool before him.

Quick to anger—that was his pa, Caleb knew—but a man of generous impulse. Twisted ankle or no, he had driven by horse-drawn sleigh over ten miles this cold December day to help Caleb celebrate a belated fifteenth birthday. A week had passed since Caleb's December third birth date, but Caleb, sure that he'd come as soon as his injury allowed him to travel, had wanted no celebration until his pa could be here. And now he had arrived, though it had meant bumping painfully over the winding, rutted lanes that passed for roads on the New Hampshire frontier of 1774.

Looking about him through the haze of tobacco smoke that shadowed the large living room of his grandfather's house, Caleb saw that the others had paid no attention to Pa's brief moment of pain. Their laughter continued, a tangible thing that warmed the spirits, just as the fire of giant oak logs that was roaring in the fireplace combined with mulled cider to keep the chill of the December day from their physical beings.

Reverend Pickels, Caleb thought, was in rare form today. In this well-furnished room, surrounded by congenial company, witticisms floated light as bubbles from the Reverend's lips. Though dressed in clerical black, this was not the same Reverend who preached damnation and doom to the meeting each Sabbath. Nor was this the stern taskmaster who strove mightily to beat into Caleb's head the learning contained in *Salmon's Historical Grammar* and *Fenning's Dictionary*. No, this placid, laughing figure, round face thrusting forward like an inquisitive owl, pudgy fingers laced over his corpulent stomach—except when one sausagelike finger would be raised to make a point—this benevolent cleric was a changed man in such company. Who then, Caleb thought, is Reverend Pickels? Is he a series of masks? It was a thought containing infinite possibilities.

Caleb looked about the room, applying the thought to others. There sat his father, raptly intent on Reverend

Pickels' words. What were his thoughts? And what of Caleb's thirteen-year-old brother Archibald, sitting in the chair at his father's left? In him Caleb could see mirrored his younger self. Both boys, Caleb knew, had inherited the saving grace of their mother's good humor. It showed on Archibald's relaxed face and in his mischievous eyes. For a moment, Caleb felt the old jealousy. Why must Archie be the one to share his folks' home? He fought down the feeling, telling himself again the reason that had been given to him. Gramp needed Caleb, as a substitute for the boy Gramp had lost. And Caleb did almost feel as if his grandparents' house was his home. It was really the only home he knew. Still, being a substitute was not quite enough. Caleb shifted his gaze from Archie, unwilling to allow this day to be dulled by envy.

Deliberately, he concentrated his attention on Uncle Bill, his father's elder brother. Uncle Bill's austere face mirrored the sober view of life that seemed ingrained in all the Starks. Now, however, his thin lips were stretched in a crooked smile that threatened to crack his face—an ultimate tribute to Reverend Pickels' drollery. Uncle Bill was a good farmer, who, together with Caleb's pa and Grandfather Page, had helped incorporate their town of Dunbarton, named for the ancestral home of the Starks in Scotland. Like Caleb's father, he had been a brave Indian fighter with Rogers' Rangers. In the French and Indian War he had distinguished himself at Crown Point and Quebec. Yet what seething thoughts must lie behind that stern face! Caleb knew these thoughts well, for he had heard them expressed by his Cousin John, now sitting next to Uncle Bill. John was about Caleb's age, but with his mouth already settling into the thin Stark line. How his eyes had flashed, earlier this winter, when Caleb had unwisely assigned to everlasting perdition General Gage and all his British lobsterback troops occupying Boston.

"Treason!" young John had cried, and Caleb could almost hear Uncle Bill's voice echoing through John's lips. Tories they were, Uncle Bill and his family. How hard it must be, Caleb thought, with his uncle's own brothers and most of the neighbors talking against the Crown. Yet Uncle Bill would stand for the right as he saw it, for that was the Stark way.

At least, with Uncle Bill and Cousin John, it was possible to know where they stood. They were no tale carriers to Governor Wentworth. Men of honor, the Starks, unlike other neighbors of Tory bent—smooth as butter on the surface until the time was right to work a disservice. Caleb looked closely about the room. Such thoughts brought to mind the Snavely family, their near neighbors opposite the north forty. There were no Snavelys present today, for that had been Caleb's wish.

He blinked as his gaze suddenly encountered the brown eyes of Prudence Davis, staring straight at him from across the room. Frilled and flounced, demurely smiling, this was not the same barefoot gamin with whom he had frolicked, gone climbing for apples, searched for bee trees—whose screams had matched his own only a few years earlier, when both had been soundly spanked for tossing gunpowder into the candle flame. Making lightning, they had called it, and it had been an exciting game, almost worth its ignominious ending. Now, beneath her gaze, he blinked, ill at ease, conscious of his pimply face, his awkward body.

"Laws, Caleb," he heard Pru say, her voice cool and amused, "you look to be hunting one of Parson Pickels' ghosts."

All eyes were turned toward him. Caleb managed a weak smile. "Hardly," he muttered. "We take small stock in such."

Reverend Pickels nodded approvingly. "Of course you don't. It's as I say, there is a lack of ghosties and such in our better homes."

Caleb advised himself to pay attention to the conversation. Evidently the good reverend was elaborating on one of his favorite themes, the supernatural.

"You would be surprised," Reverend Pickels was saying, a condescending smile on his face, "in the bottom of how many butter churns I have seen the burned outline of a flatiron. To me that's a sure sign the goodwife believes an evil spirit is in her churn. When the cream fails to granulate butter, she thinks to expel the evil spirit by throwing in a hot iron." The good reverend shook his head at the thought of such folly.

Caleb suppressed a smile as he stole a glance at his grandmother's plump face. Beneath its lacy net cap, her face reddened to the shade of a ripe love apple. As Caleb well knew, the bottom of their churn was well branded— the result of several such contacts with hot flatirons.

Gram looked relieved as the company's attention was diverted at that moment by a loud pounding at the front door. The heavy cast-iron knocker was banged sharply three times against the oak portal before Angie, the Pages' teen-age hired girl, had time to run from the kitchen to answer the peremptory summons.

"Good day, Angie." Bobbing his shaggy head, smiling broadly, young Zeb Snavely stood outside the open door, holding a cloth-wrapped parcel beneath one arm. The cold December air swept into the room, eddying the layered tobacco smoke, lending an added crackle to the blazing logs in the fireplace.

Captain Page sneezed once, twice. "Come in, Zeb. Close the door, Angie, before we all expire of the pleurisy."

Inside the room, as Angie quickly closed the door behind him, Zeb blinked to accommodate his eyes to the dim interior. About him clung the fresh smell of ozone, a reminder of the clear December day through which he had been walking. He extended his package toward Gram.

"Ma's compliments, ma'am," he said. "She thought a haunch of venison might set well with the company."

Mrs. Page smiled. "Why, thank you, Zeb. And thank your ma. Angie will take it." As the girl quickly relieved Zeb of his package and carried it to the kitchen, Mrs. Page indicated a slat-back chair near the fireplace. "Won't you rest a spell?"

Zeb, smiling his thanks, lowered his chunky form into the chair, twisting his shoulders beneath the unaccustomed restriction of his jacket.

"You do look well, Zeb," Gram said. "Your folks keeping fit?"

Zeb nodded. "They are, ma'am." He turned to look directly at Caleb, who detected the challenge in his eyes. "They wish you a happy birthday, Caleb."

Caleb felt a flush mounting to his face and cursed this easy barometer to his emotions. "That's good of them," he said, spacing his words carefully. "I thank you."

Words, polite words, he thought—and what's the good of them, but to mask a lie? It was Caleb's doing that had kept the Snavelys from this gathering, over the protests of Gram and Gramp. "Nice folks, the Snavelys," Captain Page had said. "Helping neighbors," Gram had added. But they finally had yielded. After all, it was Caleb's day.

They didn't know. They just didn't know. They hadn't lived in close contact with Zeb, worked and played and studied with him. Weasel ways, Zeb had. Beneath that smile, Caleb knew, there was hatred—hatred in the whole smiling Snavely family for the likes of the Pages and the Starks, who dared defy the King's authority. But try to tell that to Gramp, a man who believed in trusting his neighbor, never dreaming his confidences might reach the ear of Governor Wentworth. And now here was Zeb, inviting himself to Caleb's own birthday gathering. It galled Caleb, but there wasn't a thing he could do about it.

"Get Zeb a mug," Captain Page called across the room

to Caleb. "Some cider should set well after your walk, Zeb. Mulled or plain?"

"Plain, sir—if it's no trouble," Zeb replied politely.

Caleb glowered as he rose to fetch a mug. Gramp extended the cider jug as he passed beside his chair. "While you're up, you might as well go down cellar and fill the jug. It's 'most empty. And fill your pa's jug, too."

Zeb rose quickly from his chair. "I'll fill your pa's jug, Caleb."

John Stark extended the earthen jug to Zeb. "Thank ye. It does seem a mite low."

Caleb preceded Zeb down the narrow steps leading to the damp, musty depths of the earthen-floored cellar. Light filtered through one dusty window. Caleb brushed clinging strands of a cobweb from his face as he approached the cider barrel. "Let's have Pa's jug," he said to Zeb.

"I can fill it well enough," Zeb said shortly. "Fill your own."

"I just thought it might be easier—" Caleb began.

"You just thought," Zeb mimicked. "You think a lot. Mebbe you think too much."

Caleb's eyes narrowed. "I wish no trouble with you today, Zeb. Why did you come?"

Zeb glowered, his face close to Caleb's in the semidarkness. "Why wasn't I invited? Me and my folks? It rubbed Pa the wrong way, if you want to know."

Caleb kept his voice steady with an effort. "It was just that I wanted this to be a good day."

Zeb licked his lips. "Now it ain't. Is that it? Mebbe I've ruined it by being here—like a piece of stinking bad meat spoils the stew. Is that it?"

"Let's draw the cider and get back," Caleb said.

"Let's talk," Zeb demanded. "Let's get something straight. You and your family, with your high and mighty airs. You think you're too good for the Snavelys."

"I don't want to talk," Caleb said shortly. He filled his

jug with the pungent, sweet-smelling cider. "I want to get back."

Zeb grasped Caleb's arm. "You bet you want to get back. You're afraid you might hear some home truths. Well, here's one for you, free of charge. At least my ma and pa want me to live with them. That's more than some can say."

"Let go of my arm." Caleb's voice cracked as he strove to keep his temper in check.

Zeb's eyes glittered in the half-light. "My folks ain't so glad to get shut of me they farm me out. My folks—"

Caleb could stand no more. "You shut up! You—you dirty skunk's misery. Or by chowder I'll whip you good!"

Zeb pushed Caleb away from him. "You'll whup me? That'll be a cool day in Hades, you scrawny, pie-eyed marsh rat!"

He swung his empty cider jug at Caleb. Instinctively, Caleb's arm rose to protect himself. His cider jug collided in mid-air with the jug that Zeb was swinging. There was a crash of crockery. The cider liberated from Caleb's full jug doused both boys. Unheeding the sweet, sticky liquid dripping from face and clothes, the two grappled—tearing at each other's jackets, gouging and pummeling—each attempting to kick the legs out from under his opponent. A sawhorse toppled with a crash, and the two fell over it, landing full length on the dirt floor. Over and over they rolled, arms flailing.

The door at the head of the stairs flew open. Captain Page stood in the rectangle of light, a broad-shouldered figure of authority whose booming voice filled the cellar. "Boys! What in tunket's going on?"

Breathing hard, Caleb and Zeb ceased their struggle as the Captain's ominous bellow penetrated their fury. Cautiously they released their holds and rose to their feet.

"Answer me," the Captain demanded. "Or do you want me to come down there?"

"Had a little accident," Zeb called, his voice gasping and harsh. "Broke the jugs. But we're all right, sir."

"We're fine," Caleb assured him.

They slowly mounted the steps and were exposed to the full sight of the company. They were a sad-looking pair, Caleb realized—coats ripped, dripping cider, Caleb's nose bloodied, Zeb's lip cut.

Captain Page shook his head in disbelief. "What in thunderation happened?"

"I tripped," Caleb said in a low voice. "I banged into Zeb, and we both fell down and broke the jugs. I'm sorry."

Zeb nodded. "That's right. Caleb tripped."

Captain Page puffed out his full cheeks. "Tripped, you say?"

Caleb's mother quickly intervened. "Yes, dad," Molly Stark said, darting a quick glance of appeal to Gram Page. "Fifteen's an awkward age. And we *are* gathered to help Caleb celebrate his birthday. So please let's not make too much of it. He said he's sorry."

"That's right," Gram agreed, gazing firmly at her husband. "If he tripped he tripped. And there's no help for it. Now why don't you boys go out back and get cleaned up. You look a sight."

Gramp opened his mouth, took another look at Gram, closed his mouth, and contented himself with silently glowering at the culprits.

John Stark, grasping his cane, pulled himself from his chair. "I'll help you lads get clean. I don't want you tripping over each other again."

"I'm goin' home," Zeb said shortly.

"I was hoping you'd stay for dinner," Gram said. "I hate to have you going home looking such a sight. What would your ma think?"

"Special birthday dinner," Molly Stark urged. "We have room for an extra guest, don't we, Caleb?" She looked beseechingly at her son.

Caleb gulped. "Guess so." With all eyes on him, he knew well enough what he was expected to say. The words came out in a rush. "Pleased to have you stay."

Zeb's puffed lip rose in the caricature of a smile. "In that case, thank ye. Guess I will." He looked directly at Caleb, his gaze hard and cold, belying his polite acceptance.

Caleb's heart pounded and his mouth felt dry. This day wasn't turning out as he had hoped at all. Why must Zeb hang around? He looked toward his father and saw that John Stark was gravely surveying Zeb and himself.

"Let's go get washed and brushed up then," his father said, preparing to hobble after them to the wash shed. "We'll see if we can make you two presentable for civilized company."

At least Pa wasn't taken in by Zeb's smooth talk, Caleb thought. They understood each other, he and Pa. Still, Zeb's taunting words stuck in the back of his mind. Did Pa really want him around? Sometimes Caleb had nagging doubts. He'd been told often enough why he was being raised by his ma's folks—but was it the real reason?

2

☆ ☆
☆

Caleb's spirits rose as his stomach filled. It wasn't turning out to be such a bad birthday after all. Never had he eaten such a Saturday dinner. For this one day, Gram had dispensed with such usual mundane Saturday dishes as creamed dried beef and codfish with pork scraps.

Instead, on this memorable Saturday afternoon, the house was filled with the mouth-watering aroma of succulent roast goose and beef. Served on Gram's best pewter dishes and swimming in rich gravy, the tender meat was accompanied by fluffy white whipped potatoes, turnips, and pickled young butternuts; thick, crusty rye and Injun bread that Caleb spread with sweet butter and wild grape jelly; hot apple pie and pumpkin pie for dessert; real coffee, made rich with thick cream and sweetened with maple syrup.

Not until next Thanksgiving could Caleb expect such an abundance at one meal again. Not at Christmas, for Gram and Gramp, like most of their neighbors, shied away from making much of Christmas—a carry-over from early Puritan austerity; not at the New Year, for country folk in New Hampshire did not condone such New Year celebrations as Caleb heard were common among the New York people.

Just as well, Caleb thought. If he were to eat so heartily as a regular diet, he was sure his stomach would burst. He looked down the table at the surfeited diners taking their ease, the men puffing contentedly at their pipes.

Beside him, Caleb's mother smiled as she lightly touched his arm. "Good birthday, son?"

Caleb gave an answering grin. "The best."

"I hope it was worth the wait of a week past your natural birth date," his mother said. She raised her eyebrows in mock exasperation as she glanced across the table toward her husband. "Your pa couldn't have picked a worse time to sprain his ankle."

John Stark shook his head. "I did it on purpose, of course —being so natural mean." He winked at Caleb.

Caleb smiled at their gentle banter. "I would have waited no matter how long. It wouldn't be a proper celebration without you."

Gramp's booming voice added its endorsement. "Well said, lad."

Reverend Pickels clinked spoon on mug. "Hear hear."

Molly Stark looked pleased. "We couldn't do much in the way of presents this year, Caleb. But you do like the shirt?"

Caleb nodded, momentarily speechless as the warmth of his family's affection suddenly tightened his throat and threatened to bring tears to his eyes.

His mother smiled. "It does seem to fit. You grow so, Caleb, 'tis hard to know your size."

"The fit couldn't be better," Gram observed. Unthinkingly, she added, "A good happenstance you had it to wear, Caleb, after your tumble."

Across the table, Archie guffawed. "Some tumble."

John Stark, sitting beside his younger son, silenced him with a hard glance, then looked thoughtfully toward Zeb, sitting at the far end of the table. Noting a smirk on that lad's face, he glanced toward Caleb, who was twisting uneasily in his chair, and made a sudden decision. Rising painfully from his chair, he excused himself from the table. "There is some business Caleb and I must attend to," he said in answer to his wife's questioning look. His voice was surprisingly soft as he spoke to Caleb. "Will you accompany me, son?"

Caleb nodded, puzzled, and also excused himself. Leaning on a cane and limping ahead to the guest room off the main hall where they were to spend the night, his father closed the door and motioned to a small brocaded chair. Caleb slowly seated himself. The puzzlement caused by these abrupt actions showed plain on his face.

John Stark, leaning forward on his cane, faced Caleb. Though of medium stature, he seemed to the seated lad to be a towering figure. His trim, well-muscled body belied his forty-six years, as did his luxuriant shock of hair, barely dotted with gray. Only the face, Caleb thought, showed his age. Looking up, Caleb felt that the face of his father was lined with untold miseries and hardships. It was a long, stern face with thin lips that Caleb knew offered visible proof of his father's close-mouthed character. Looking into John Stark's ice-blue eyes, deeply sunk under shaggy eyebrows, Caleb had the feeling that these eyes could pierce to the core of truth in a man.

They now were demanding the truth from Caleb. "What happened down cellar?"

And Caleb told the truth—haltingly, unwillingly—for he knew that his pa would settle for nothing less.

When Caleb had finished, John Stark stood looking down at his son for a long moment, and the boy saw his blue eyes soften. Then the father sat down slowly upon the bed, nodding his head, wordless. Yes, he seemed to say, I can see how it would be. He looked at Caleb with compassion. Not a word was spoken, but for Caleb this was a moment of union with his father—and an answer to the question that had plagued his boyhood. In this moment he knew that he was loved.

At length John Stark spoke, his words measured and slow. He took the blame to himself for not fully explaining Caleb's upbringing. He and Caleb's mother had thought they'd told the boy all he needed to know—but evidently it hadn't been enough. "I don't offer excuses for my shortcomings," Stark said. "I am the way I am, and God knows that's far from perfect. You must make allowances, for my life has been filled with much action and—I fear—little thought."

Caleb nodded encouragement. Who in the colony didn't know of his pa, a man who seemed marked for greatness from early youth? Snatched by raiding Indians from his family farm on the Merrimack River, he had endured a march to the St. Francis Indian village in Canada and had become a favorite of his captors when he had courageously defied them. It was common knowledge how Pa had run the gantlet that was the usual fate of captives. But instead of running as fast as possible between the double line of

Indians, he had wrested a stick from an Indian in the gant-let and belabored the savage with his own cudgel. It was told that his pa had been given a hoe by his captors but had thrown the hoe to the ground, knowing that Indians considered hoeing to be women's work.

The tribe honored courage. It had wanted to adopt him as one of its own warriors, but John Stark's thoughts had always been of home. Finally ransomed from the tribe—for an Indian pony, as Pa was fond of telling—he had come home, a hero of sorts and a fit candidate to join Rogers' Rangers in the French and Indian War.

He had gained the rank of Captain in the Rangers. Caleb's father didn't speak much of his career as a soldier, but Caleb knew he had led his men in the terrible fighting at Ticonderoga, Crown Point, Louisburg, and Quebec.

In the midst of the war he had come on furlough and had married Molly Page. Caleb had heard that romantic tale often enough, and he knew that he had been born in Captain Page's house while his pa was off again to the wars.

It was during this period too that Grandpa Stark had died, leaving the family farm in the care of young Captain Stark. Small wonder that when the surrender of Canada in 1760 ended the war, John Stark called a halt to his military career and concentrated on farming the family acres. He'd seen enough action to fill two lifetimes for the average man.

With all that responsibility, Caleb told himself, Pa couldn't have any time to pamper a tiny mite of a son. He was a busy man. So Caleb's reason told him. But a boy's emotions don't yield too well to reason. Caleb needed his pa. He was glad that now, starting his sixteenth year, his pa had finally made the effort to pull them closer together.

"You must remember," John Stark was saying, "your Grandpa Page feels things deep. That's the way sometimes with jolly folks. They laugh, but laughing may cover a hurt. Do I speak plain, son?"

Caleb nodded. "I know." How well he knew, for he had inherited the same sensitivity. But that he kept to himself.

His pa looked beyond Caleb, to a distant time etched in his memory. "You know all I'm about to say, but you must realize how important your staying here is to Gramp. You took the place of his boy who died in battle at Crown Point—his oldest boy, Caleb, Jr., the one for whom you're named. It was a bad battle. I was there with the Rangers, as was young Caleb—a Ranger ensign. He fought well. And he died. That was in January of fifty-seven, over a year before I married your ma. My dad and I knew Captain Page well. We'd all worked together, incorporating this town of Dunbarton.

"I saw when next I was home on furlough how the news of his boy's death had aged Captain Page. His clothes seemed to hang on him. His voice would trail off with a thought half expressed. Never have I seen a man so will away his life. Always before so full of wit—but now the spark was almost gone. Mrs. Page would jolly him. She wasn't so down as the Captain—she being his second wife, and Caleb not her own son. She felt his death, of course, but she rallied faster than the old man. Your ma, too, tried her best to put some life in him. They'd pamper him, and make him dainties, but he'd leave them 'most untouched."

Caleb's eyes were wide. "I didn't realize. I knew—but not that he was so bad off."

"I should have spoken sooner," his father said. "You saved him, Caleb. You were the miracle that saved the old man. After I married Molly and you were born, it was just like blowing new life into him. Your ma was staying with her folks then, of course, for I was at the wars, and Captain Page was the man of the house. And there you were, Caleb, like a son reborn to him, crowing and gurgling in your cradle. The years dropped away. He laughed and joked and ate his fill. And this house again became a pleasurable place. You did that, Caleb."

"You make me sound important, Pa."

"So you are. The most important thing in your Gramp's life. Do you see how it was, when the fighting was over and I had to take your ma away to our farm in Derryfield, what a decision we had to make about you? You are our first born. Of course we love you. It was just like leaving a piece of herself for your ma to leave you behind. But your Gramp needed you—really needed you. And we were young and trusted we'd have more of a family.

"We decided to make the sacrifice. Captain Page is a well-to-do man, even though he does prefer living on the edge of the wilderness. We knew he'd give you the best sort of upbringing."

"He has," Caleb assured him. "Writing, ciphering, and such. He's seen to that. He and Reverend Pickels."

"We knew he would. But even so, we felt we were making a big sacrifice. We were younger then. Now we know it's you that made the sacrifice—and you weren't even asked."

"It's all right, Pa," Caleb said earnestly. "Now I understand."

John Stark shook his head. "It will never be all right. But at least you know the straight truth—and all the Zebs in the world will have a harder time hurting you."

"No reason for hurt," Caleb said. "I'm glad we talked, Pa."

"We should have talked so years ago," his father said gruffly, "though maybe now at your age you truly understand." With an effort, he raised himself from his seat on the bed. Leaning on the cane he held in one hand, he grasped Caleb's arm with the other. "By the by, if anybody asks what we talked of in this room, you can say we discussed your trip to Epsom, to see Captain McClary." His thin lips formed the suggestion of a smile. "That is, if you care to go."

Caleb brightened. The Captain was a particular favorite of his. "You told me of no such trip. Of course I want to go. When?"

"Sooner the better, I'd say. The Captain's courier stopped at the farm just before your ma and I were to set out for your birthday doings. I told him a man in my condition couldn't make the trip to Epsom—but the messenger said it was important for McClary to see me. I promised to send an alternate."

"I'll do my best," Caleb assured him.

"You'll have to watch yourself," his father said. "Weather's treacherous, for all it's been a mild winter. There's no road passable for a horse from here to Epsom this time of year, so you'll have to walk a good day's journey. By rights, you should have someone go with you."

"How about Archie?"

"Too young. Give him another year or so. Your cousin John would be a good companion, but his pa's dead set against us of late. I doubt he'd let him go."

Caleb shook his head. " 'Twouldn't be smart to have men of such a bent around the Captain. Specially since he's so powerful eager to talk with you."

"Something probably *is* afoot," John Stark agreed. "Still, a traveling companion needn't hear any talk you'd have with the Captain. The main thing is protection on the trail —someone with a strong arm, and handy with a musket."

He paused. By the look in John Stark's eye, Caleb surmised the same name had popped into his pa's mind that came to his. "You thinking of Zeb?" he asked.

His father nodded, a half smile momentarily lighting his face. "I was."

Caleb shook his head. "We'd not get along."

"On the trail you'd have to get along."

"I don't trust him," Caleb said in a low voice.

)23(

"All my life I've dealt with men I don't trust," John Stark said.

It was obvious to Caleb that John Stark didn't fully see through Zeb's deceitful nature. It was equally obvious that there was no one else available at such short notice whom his pa would approve to accompany him on his journey. And he did want to go. There was an urgency to the Captain's message that excited him.

"If you think so—" Caleb began. Then, with sudden decision, he said, "Put it to him if you like, Pa."

Zeb proved eager to go, once the journey was outlined to him. A bit too eager, Caleb thought, reasoning that it couldn't be his company that Zeb hankered for. The lad's eagerness must be all of a piece for his reason for insinuating himself into the Stark household this day. Big events must truly be brewing to provoke such interest in their affairs by the Snavely family.

Caleb felt a tingle run up his spine. This journey promised to be an adventure.

3
☆ ☆
☆

The next day was crisp and clear. A good day for a trip, Caleb thought, as he followed behind Zeb on snowshoes shaped like squash seeds. He was glad to be traveling on such a day, although he would have preferred more agreeable company. The two boys had exchanged scarcely a dozen words since meeting at Caleb's house at dawn. Now, as they flapped their way over soft snow toward the trail that led to the great woods, Caleb warned himself that he must be careful. No telling what thoughts were concealed behind Zeb's sullen face. At least, he'll do me no bodily harm, Caleb assured himself, feeling certain that Zeb also was eager to reach Epsom and hear Captain McClary's news.

Meanwhile, he would not let Zeb entirely spoil the pleasure of this day. He breathed deep the clear, crisp air, savoring the ozone mingling with resinous scent of the evergreen forest that lay ahead of them. Spiked tops of towering firs were etched against a clear blue sky by slanting rays of early morning sun. Tree limbs, weighted by snow, drooped downward. The trees looked like a company of drab mourners, except that the sun, sparkling on their snow-weighted branches, added a festive touch.

As they followed the drifted trail into the woods, the cold strengthened. Caleb was grateful now for the warmth provided by his frontiersman's outfit of coonskin hat, fringed leather jacket, buckskin gaiters, and high leather moccasins. He had protested this backwoods outfit at first, but his father had insisted. Noting that Zeb was dressed in almost identical fashion, Caleb wondered if he also had been given some parental advice.

Both boys had heavy flintlock muskets slung over their shoulders, and each carried a powder horn and a bullet pouch suspended from two rawhide straps crossing over the chest. Each had a long hunting knife hung from his belt.

Caleb felt unwilling admiration for Zeb's ability to follow the snow-drifted trail. It was a familiar one to both boys, for they had walked it each summer on their way to the fishing grounds on the Merrimack River. But now the trail merged with the snow-covered forest floor, and a true woodsman's instinct was needed to follow its twisting turns. Caleb recognized the height of land they were passing, as the ground began to slope downward toward the river. Traveling was easier on this downhill grade.

Soon the boys reached the winding Merrimack, which

appeared to be frozen solid from bank to bank. They paused, studying the seemingly firm surface.

"How's it look to you?" Caleb asked.

Zeb shrugged. "Dunno till we test it."

Cautiously they slid down the bank onto the river ice. They shuffled slowly forward on their snowshoes, using their musket butts to test the surface of the ice ahead of them. Both knew that the twisting current of the rocky river caused air holes in the ice—thin spots where the water did not freeze thickly. These air holes, covered with a thin layer of snow, could become traps for the unwary. Both boys had heard tales of travelers who had gone through such soft spots and had been sucked under the ice by the river's rushing current. Usually the bodies of these victims were not recovered until the spring thaw.

Slowly they inched their way across the ice, probing with their musket butts every foot of the way. At midstream, Zeb's musket poked a hole through a thin layer of snow, and they had a frightening glimpse of black, rushing water.

"Easy," Caleb warned. "It's not a fit day for a swim."

Zeb grunted. Cautiously, the two backed off, probing for firmer ice. They found safe footing a few yards upstream and proceeded slowly. No more air holes were discovered, but Caleb did not breathe easily until they had reached solid footing on the far bank. There he made a mock bow to the river.

"Good day, Mistress Merrimack. We'll not be your guests quite yet."

Zeb laughed shortly. "Were you worried?"

Caleb nodded. "I'll admit it. For a minute there, I was indeed."

"Not I," said Zeb. "It takes more than a winter river crossing to affright me."

Caleb looked at him closely. Zeb probably spoke the truth, he thought. "Good for you, Zeb," he said lightly.

"Since you're so good a guide, I'll also let you lead the way across the Suncook River into Epsom."

"That ditch? I could broad jump it, if need be."

Caleb did not reply. There was no humor in Zeb, and Caleb felt the futility of attempting to maintain a friendly conversation. Silently the boys toiled up the steep riverbank and into the woods beyond. We're almost halfway to the Captain's house, Caleb thought. His spirits rose. The trip promised to be an easy one from this point on.

As sunlight brightened the snow ahead, Caleb raised his eyes to the small patch of blue sky visible through the interlocking pine branches overhead. And there was the panther! A shaft of sunlight touched its reddish-brown fur as it crouched high in a tall pine tree. Every inch of its compact frame seemed to ripple with muscles. Caleb stared at its huge cat face, and the animal steadily returned his gaze, unmoving except for a slight twitching of its long tail.

"Watch out!" Caleb called softly as Zeb, ahead of him, approached the tree. Zeb paused, and as his gaze followed the direction of Caleb's pointing finger he too saw the beast.

Involuntarily he retreated a step, then glared at Caleb. "You scared of a bobcat?" he demanded.

"Bobcat!" Caleb exclaimed. "You ever see a bobcat with a long tail like that? That's a painter, mister," he said, using the common name for panther.

Slowly Zeb raised his musket, which was already loaded, and poured powder from his powder horn into the pan. He leveled the musket at the big cat. The panther, sensing danger, drew back its lips, exposing long curved fangs. It growled deep in its throat.

Zeb took careful aim.

"He won't bother us if we leave him alone," Caleb said desperately.

Zeb ignored him. His finger tightened on the trigger. There was a flash and a loud report, as the heavy one-ounce slug from Zeb's musket tore into the hindquarters of the beast.

The panther leaped into the air, screaming in pain, blood gushing from its wound. It landed snarling on its feet at the base of the tree and spun about to face the two boys. It crouched low, belly to the ground, tail switching savagely, jaws open, exposing its terrible teeth. It seemed ready to spring.

Quickly Caleb primed his loaded musket and aimed it at the panther. He fired, and the heavy ball tore into the animal's shoulder, the force of the impact knocking it on its side and rolling it over in the blood-soaked snow. But the panther struggled to its feet and again faced the boys. Although one front paw now hung limp, the great cat still seemed full of fight.

Caleb saw with dismay that Zeb was rushing into the woods at the side of the trail. "Zeb!" he called sharply.

"Gotta reload," Zeb called back. "Be ready in a minute!"

A minute might be too late, Caleb thought, but he had no time to remonstrate. He dared not take his eyes off the panther, now crouched, every muscle tensed, as if preparing to leap straight toward him.

Frantically, Caleb poured powder and inserted a ball into the barrel of his musket. As he tamped down the charge with his long ramrod, he saw the big cat gather itself to spring. No time now to prime his musket. No time even to remove the ramrod. He must rely on an old Ranger trick his father had taught him. Quickly he struck the butt of his musket on the ground, hoping to bring enough powder into the pan so that the musket would prime itself.

He swung the musket to his shoulder and fired point-blank as the panther launched itself in a powerful spring. Straight toward him it leaped, fangs bared. There was a loud report as the musket fired the long ramrod, deadlier than a musket ball, into the panther's chest. It struck the animal in mid-air, deflecting its spring. The boy, awkwardly sidestepping on his snowshoes, paused a safe distance away from the panther, which now thrashed about in its death agony.

Soon it was still. Caleb cautiously approached and looked with awe at the great cat, which in death still seemed to snarl defiance. Caleb's ramrod, protruding from its chest, was bent. He made no effort to retrieve it.

Hearing Zeb slowly approach behind him, Caleb turned to face the boy. Zeb's face was pale. "He's dead?" Zeb asked in a husky voice.

Caleb stepped aside so that the other could have a good look at the animal. "What do you think?" he asked shortly.

As Zeb looked at the dead beast, his small eyes became rounder than Caleb had ever before seen them. "A monstrous critter," Zeb observed, his voice almost a whisper.

"Not so monstrous, lying there dead," Caleb said. "Jumping at me through the air—that's when he looked monstrous."

Zeb didn't meet Caleb's gaze. "I was coming to help," he said defensively. "I had my musket all reloaded. But you got him before I had a chance to fire."

Caleb could not conceal the anger in his voice. "Sure, you'd take good care of him. But I'd probably been mangled some in the meantime."

"You think I didn't want to help?" Zeb burst out.

Caleb looked at him steadily, forcing Zeb's eyes to meet his. "I don't know," he said at length. "That's a thought I'd wish to harbor 'gainst no one."

Zeb's confidence was slowly returning. "Don't harbor it 'gainst me, then," he said in a low voice. He prodded the dead animal with a snowshoe. "Want to skin out this cat?"

Caleb shook his head. "No time. Not if we're to make Epsom by nightfall."

"It's a prime skin," Zeb observed. " 'Twouldn't take long to skin it out. Make a nice wall hanging or rug."

"I want no reminder of that painter on my wall or floor," Caleb said decisively. "I'll remember him plain enough without that."

Zeb looked down covetously at the painter. "I could take the skin home with me."

"No, Zeb. I shot him. He's my painter. And I want him left right there."

"I'm not denying he's yours," Zeb grumbled. "It's just that I hate to see a good skin go to waste."

"If that painter had got to me, you could have my skin for a trophy," Caleb observed. "That'd make a pretty sight, nailed up on your wall."

Zeb looked uncomfortable. "That's no way to talk. When you get home, I hope you don't give no fool idea to your folks that I let you down."

"Why should I?" Caleb asked innocently. "Do *you* think you let me down?"

"Course I didn't," Zeb protested loudly.

"Then there's naught to worry you," Caleb assured him. "Let's go. If you're ready."

"I'm ready," Zeb said. "Will you lead the way?"

"You lead. I feel safer when you're in front of me."

Zeb wheeled to face him. "Now what do you mean by that?"

"Why, just that you're such a good guide," Caleb said softly. "What else would I mean?"

Zeb opened his mouth to speak, then thought better of it, shut his lips tightly, and started down the trail. He set a fast pace, but Caleb had no trouble keeping close behind him.

Not another word was spoken during the remaining ten miles to the Suncook River. As Zeb had said earlier, the stream was narrow at this point and presented no hazard. They were soon on the opposite bank, toiling up the slope leading toward Epsom and the farm of Captain Mc-Clary.

The sun was setting as they reached the end of the forest trail. It sparkled on the snow-covered crests of distant peaks. As the boys walked across wintry fields toward the road leading to Captain McClary's farmhouse, it cast their shadows ahead of them—two elongated, splintery figures, snowshoeing across the snow.

It was the quiet time of day. Scarcely a sound disturbed the stillness. How peaceful Epsom seemed on the surface, Caleb thought. How deceptively quiet. Remembering the reason for their visit, he thought of the explosive emotions that lay just below the surface in Epsom, as in his own town of Dunbarton and in so many other quiet little towns in the colonies.

Pointing to a solidly built farmhouse visible over the next ridge, he spoke for the first time since they had resumed their trip. "That's Captain McClary's farm."

"About time," Zeb grumbled. "I hope he sets a good table."

Tired as he was, Caleb quickened his pace. He was hungry too. But more than hunger was driving him now. He felt a rising excitement as they neared the house. Soon he would hear the news that his father's friend considered so important.

4

The boys removed their snowshoes and leaned them against the McClary farmhouse. Caleb rapped on the heavy oak door of the kitchen. A trodden path led here, but no footprints marred the snow at the front door. He smiled, thinking of the Pages' front door at home, unused during the winter months except for special occasions. They cleared the front path for my birthday celebration, he suddenly remembered. He hadn't really thought of that before, but now the memory brought a flush of pleasure. That had certainly been a special occasion.

Caleb gulped as he heard heavy footsteps approaching inside the house. Would the Captain remember him? It had been two years since McClary had seen him. And Caleb knew that he had changed in two years' time. I'll introduce myself, he thought. I'll say, "I'm John Stark's son, Caleb. And this is—" His mind went blank. He knew his traveling companion's name as well as he knew his own. Yet he could not, for the life of him, remember it at this moment. I must truly be nervous, he thought.

The door opened, and Caleb looked up at all six feet six inches of Captain McClary. He opened his mouth to introduce himself, but before he could make a sound his hand was seized in the hamlike hand of the Captain and a booming voice proclaimed, "By mighty! It's Caleb! Come in, come in, lad, you and your friend. Ye look cold as a lamb's tongue."

For the first time, Caleb realized how cold he was. Bone chilled, he thought, once he entered the kitchen and felt the warm air surround him. It sent sharp prickles through his ears and fingers. He shivered slightly. The smell of a savory stew simmering on the hearth set his stomach to rumbling. He was cold and hungry, but he had pushed all such feelings from his mind until he had reached his destination. Now, in the friendly warmth of the McClary kitchen, his tension relaxed.

"Don't think I know your friend," the Captain said, waiting to be introduced.

Suddenly the name that Caleb knew as well as his own came to his lips. "Zeb Snavely," he said. "Zeb, I'd like you to meet Captain McClary."

Zeb gave his warmest smile and pumped the Captain's hand. "Good to meet you, sir."

"Pleasure," the Captain murmured. He looked inquiringly at Caleb. "Your pa get my message?"

Caleb nodded. "I'm here in his stead. His ankle's that twisted, he can scarce hobble."

"A serious hurt?" the Captain asked.

"Serious for Pa," Caleb replied. "It frets him to sit idle. He says time will mend him good as new."

"Bid him have patience then," the Captain said. "Easy advice to give, but hard to take, I know. It was good of you lads to come in his stead. It's a long trip, and you look done in." He gave a short laugh. "About how I feel myself."

The Captain did indeed look weary. He had evidently been doing farm labor, for he was dressed in his working clothes: leather breeches and a coarse jacket that reached down halfway to the knees. His long hair was tousled.

"Are we keeping you from table?" Caleb asked.

"No, no," the Captain said. "We'll eat together. I'm behind time, for I had the oxen out all day, hauling wood. On my last trip from the woodlot, I shot a yearling buck and had to skin him out."

"We did a little shooting ourselves on the way here," Caleb said. Zeb shifted his feet uncomfortably.

"Get a deer?" the Captain asked.

"Shot a painter," Caleb told him, trying to keep his voice casual.

"A painter!" the Captain exclaimed. He turned to the plump middle-aged woman bending over the kettles on the hearth. You hear that, Mrs. McClary? The lads shot a painter!"

Her eyes opened wide. "Land o' mercy!" The long wooden spoon with which she had been stirring the stew hung motionless in her hand.

"Shot him dead?" the Captain demanded.

"Deader 'n a doornail," Caleb replied.

"I shot him first," Zeb said quickly.

"Got him real riled up too," Caleb added.

Captain McClary, noting the flush that spread over Zeb's face, said quickly, "I'll have to hear all about it, but right now we could all do with some vittles. Meet my wife, boys. Mrs. McClary, you've met Caleb—John Stark's boy. And this is his friend, Zeb Snavely."

Mrs. McClary smiled. "Glad to see you."

A girl that Caleb judged to be about four years old peeked out from behind Mrs. McClary's full skirt and looked up wide-eyed at the boys. Her mother patted the girl's blonde hair. "You want to meet our guests, too, don't ye, honey? This is Margaret." The little girl ducked quickly back behind her mother's skirts.

The Captain laughed and pointed to the kitchen doorway. There, several other children, standing in a large room beyond the kitchen, cautiously inspected the guests. "Shy as mice, the lot of them," the Captain said. "Don't know where they get it from. That littlest one's Nancy, with 'Lizabeth holding her, and those are my two youngest boys, John and Bill. There's two big brothers in the barn, doing chores. Say 'howdy' to our guests, young'uns."

The children bobbed their heads in greeting and clustered closer together.

"You start bedding down," Mrs. McClary ordered them. She turned to Caleb and Zeb. "We've all supped, save for the Captain. If you'll set yourselves, I'll dish out some spoon meat. Then I'll see to the young'uns." She plucked Margaret away from her skirt and motioned toward the doorway. "You join the others, Margaret. I'll be right along."

Mrs. McClary ladled steaming venison stew into a large wooden serving bowl. Caleb and Zeb left their muskets leaning against the wall and seated themselves next to the Captain at a long table near the hearth. Mrs. McClary set pewter mugs, plates, spoons, and sharp wooden-handled knives before each of them and placed the bowl of stew and a loaf of bread on the table. "Help yourselves," she said.

Caleb and Zeb needed no urging. They gulped the tasty stew as if they hadn't eaten for days. The Captain's appetite seemed almost as hearty. There was no conversation as they ate the stew and sopped up the gravy with slices of thick-crusted bread.

Mrs. McClary looked on approvingly. "We don't drink tea in this house," she said. "Not since the tax trouble. But I do have coffee."

The Captain wrinkled his nose. "Such as it is."

Mrs. McClary, paying him no attention, poured dark brown liquid into the boys' mugs. Caleb took a sip. It was bitter, but it warmed his insides.

The Captain's mug was filled from the cider jug. He took a gulp and smacked his lips. "Now there's a drink that does a man some good. I refuse to do penance by drinking that other stuff." His wife looked hurt for a moment, but smiled as the Captain added, "Mrs. McClary may not hold with drinking cider, but she does cook up a good batch of boiled cider applesass. My nose tells me that's what's at hand—a sasser of applesass."

Caleb's nose had conveyed the same message, as he sniffed the aromatic steam issuing from an iron kettle on the hearth.

The sass was as good as the Captain had predicted. After serving two helpings, Mrs. McClary excused herself to bed down her children in the next room. She flushed with pleasure as her husband's booming voice followed her. "Did I pick a good cook for wife, lads, or did I not? The minute I set eyes on Elizabeth McCrillis, I knew I'd eat well all my days."

His wife turned for a moment before leaving the room. "When you first set eyes on me, I was a great hand to burn everything I touched."

"True," the Captain agreed. "Lucky for you I preferred my vittles well done. But see how ye've progressed over the years! I know the look of a good cook when I see one."

His wife smiled. "And credit me with knowing the look of a good man, Mr. McClary," she said softly.

The Captain beamed as his wife left the room. "She has the gift of sweet talk," he confided. " 'Tis a McCrillis trait."

He pushed his chair back from the table and patted his ample stomach. "Let me light up," he said, "and then we can chat." Filling the bowl of his long-stemmed clay pipe from the tobacco jar, he extracted a hot coal from the fireplace with a pair of tongs and lighted his pipe. Resuming his place at the table, he puffed deliberately for a moment. A pungent haze of tobacco smoke swirled about him. Slowly he removed the pipe and looked first at Caleb and then at Zeb. "I wish to speak out," he said at length. "Are all three of us of a like mind?"

Caleb glanced at Zeb, who twisted uncomfortably in his chair.

Captain McClary frowned. "Well? What say you?"

Zeb cleared his throat. "If you please, sir, we all want to see the colonies prosper. There I'm sure we're of a like mind."

"I can't argue that," the Captain said impatiently. "The question is, how do we prosper—by defying the King's Parliament or by behaving like slaves?"

"I am no slave," Zeb said stiffly, "nor do I defy my King."

Captain McClary looked at him solemnly. "I see. I take it then that we are not truly of a like mind. But one thing I must make very clear to ye. I don't defy King George. I cling to the hope that he's a just man. It's his false advisers in the Parliament I quarrel with." He looked at Caleb. "And you, boy?"

"You know my pa," Caleb said simply. "Is that answer enough?"

Captain McClary's features relaxed. "It is. Your Pa and I have been to hell and back together." He studied Zeb for a long moment. "If ye hold loyalist views, it's to your credit you've spoken straight out."

Zeb looked properly modest, and Caleb clenched his teeth. He knew well enough that Zeb had no choice but to proclaim himself, before Caleb had the chance. At any rate, he thought, now the Captain knows—and that's the main thing.

"Loyalist or no," McClary continued, "I'll speak to the point, for the time is past for caution." He looked directly at Caleb. "That's the message I mean to convey to your pa. The day is soon coming when we all must stand up and be counted."

"I don't understand—" Caleb began.

The Captain silenced him with a gesture. "You will soon enough. It's been building and building, ever since the tea was dumped in Boston Harbor."

He told them facts they all knew, but in the Captain's steady, unemotional recital they assumed a grave new importance. The destruction of tea in Boston Harbor, in protest of the tea tax, had aroused the King and Parliament to furious action. England had vowed that the seditious rebels of Boston town must be taught a lesson. Boston would serve as a warning to the rest of the colonies.

Captain McClary looked directly at Zeb. "As ye know, since June the port of Boston's been blockaded by British ships. There's no commerce in that port. Over three thousand British troops fill the town. They're quartered in private homes. Town meeting's abolished. Government's in the hands of Tories. Boston is a ghost town. How can ye pledge your allegiance to a country that treats us thus?"

"All they want is payment for the tea," Zeb said sullenly.

"Indeed," said Captain McClary, "and do ye really believe that? All they want is for us to grovel on our bellies and beg forgiveness." He smashed his great fist on the table, making the dishes jump. "No, by Heaven, we will not grovel!" With an effort, he controlled his voice. "How little they know us! Yet they fought with us against the French and Indians. There are many who'll attest to our fighting qualities. But still Parliament thinks us country bumpkins, to quail and quake at a harsh word." The Captain turned to Caleb. "I think the time's coming when they'll know us better. It almost came when General Gage's troops seized the Charlestown powder. But then the time was not quite right. Remember, Caleb?"

Caleb nodded. He did indeed remember the wave of anger that had resulted from British seizure of Massachusetts gunpowder from the Charlestown powder house. Wild rumors of armed conflict had filled the colonies, and many thought that war finally had come. Thousands of armed patriots had converged at Cambridge, ready for battle—only to be told by their cautious leaders that there had been no conflict and that Gage had acted within his rights as Governor.

"We were still treading soft then," Captain McClary said. "That was September. Now it's December, and this time our tread won't be so light."

"Trouble's brewing?" Caleb asked.

"There's reason to think so," the Captain replied. He turned as the outer door opened and two boys in long work jackets entered. Caleb thought one to be in his early teens and the other a year or so younger.

"Looks like chores are over," the Captain said. "Boys, I want you to meet Caleb Stark and Zeb Snavely. Caleb and Zeb, these are my boys, Jim and Andrew."

As the four self-consciously acknowledged the introduction, Caleb noted the quick transition the Captain had made from fiery rebel to home-loving farmer. It was a trait that reminded him of his father. Perhaps the feelings went together. Both men were willing to risk being called rebels because of the love they held for their land and family.

Caleb mulled this thought over as he and Zeb sat about the table with the McClarys later that evening, in deepening dusk relieved by soft candlelight. The conversation was desultory—of farming, local doings, death, and marriage. But underlying all their talk was an awareness of approaching crisis. Trouble was coming. Captain McClary had said as much. Caleb wondered what form it would take, then bade himself be patient. The Captain would tell him when the time was right.

Late in the evening those in the room heard a horse approach on the gallop. There was a jingle of harness outside the house and then a great pounding on the kitchen door, as if their impatient visitor would drive a fist through the panel.

Captain McClary was at the door in three long strides. As he threw it open, the rider stepped inside—cheeks flushed with the cold, eyes bloodshot, greatcoat powdered with snow flung up by his horse's hoofs.

"Jim Patton!" McClary exclaimed.

"Aye, what's left of me," the rider croaked. "I must speak to you in private, Captain."

The Captain looked about him, frowning. "Small privacy here. Come into the shed." Quickly he led the man out a door at the side of the kitchen.

Mrs. McClary busied herself with quilting squares, frowning over each stitch. Zeb and Caleb were silent, ears attuned to the low voices in the shed, frequently interspersed by the Captain's loud exclamations.

That news didn't take long in the telling, Caleb thought, as the rider hustled from the shed, across the kitchen, and out the door, scarcely glancing at the others in the room. Captain McClary stood at the open door, as the rider leaped on his horse and continued down the road.

As the Captain re-entered the kitchen, closing the door behind him, his wife looked up calmly from her sewing. "The poor man could have used something warm in his stomach."

"I asked him," the Captain replied, "but he said there's no time. He'll be all night spreading the word Paul Revere brought this day from Boston." He seated himself at the table and spoke directly to Caleb. "I'll speak out, for I feel the time for secrecy is past. The news soon will be common knowledge." He took a deep breath. "Two regiments of redcoats prepare to leave Boston. They mean to sail up our coast and seize the powder in Fort William and Mary."

"Seize it!" Zeb exclaimed. "Seize what they already own? William and Mary's a British fort."

The Captain glowered. "I have no time for niceties of speech. This is powder needed by New Hampshire, and they aim to keep it from us."

"You knew this might happen?" Caleb asked.

"I did," McClary acknowledged. "There were rumors. It's all part of a British plan that's been long in the making. Today Revere rode to Major Sullivan in Durham. He brought a copy of an order obtained by the Committee of Safety in Boston, an order passed by the King in Council that forbids export of gunpowder and military stores to America. That means if Gage can get his hands on our powder, we're at his mercy—for the colonies make no gunpowder worthy of the name."

Caleb saw that Zeb was struggling to erase a triumphant smile. When Zeb spoke to the Captain, his expression was suitably serious. "Then, sir, it seemed they have the upper hand."

The Captain's eyes narrowed. "That would seem to be the very situation."

Caleb felt a growing excitement. "Not if we can get to that powder first!"

The Captain leaned forward and clapped him on the

shoulder. "By mighty, that's the talk I expect from John Stark's son!"

Zeb leaped to his feet. "You're talking rebellion! To take the King's powder from his own fort—" He turned desperately to the Captain's wife. "Don't you see what this means?"

Mrs. McClary continued to keep her eyes fixed on her sewing. Her voice was calm. "We all know what it means, lad."

"There's a gathering tomorrow in Portsmouth," the Captain said. "Can ye make me a light meal for the road, Mrs. McClary?"

His wife nodded.

Caleb's eyes gleamed. "Could ye make that two meals?"

Mrs. McClary looked inquiringly at her husband.

"I have no right to place you in danger, Caleb," the Captain said. "You're not yet of age."

"My pa knew greater danger than this at my age," Caleb reminded him.

"True," the Captain conceded. "There are some that grow up faster than others." He considered a moment. " 'Twould do no harm, I dare say. In Portsmouth, you could see what happens and report back to your pa."

A wide grin creased Caleb's face. "Thank ye, Cap'n. I'll be no trouble."

Zeb's glare was a challenge. "I s'pose," he said, "ye wouldn't care to have me along too?"

McClary regarded him coolly. "Why not? I have a horse for each, and I'm sure Mrs. McClary can provision us."

Caleb's eyes opened wide in disbelief.

The Captain smiled at him. "Calm yourself, Caleb. Our young Tory can do us no mischief. And I'm sure none is planned."

Zeb looked uncomfortable.

"He can list the names of those gathered in Portsmouth," Caleb protested.

"So he can," the Captain agreed, "and so much the better, I say. Look sharp and long at tomorrow's assemblage, Zeb, for every man jack of us will deem it high honor to be put on the King's black list."

"If that's your wish, sir—" Zeb spoke through clenched teeth.

5

The three riders were up and away shortly before dawn, passing through a cold white countryside that wavered beneath shifting gray mist. Though the winding dirt roads were drifted with snow that concealed dangerous patches of ice, traveling was comparatively easy. As Captain McClary remarked, 1774 was the mildest December in his memory. Their mounts, sure-footed and used to the winter trails, made good time in traveling the twenty-odd miles to Major Sullivan's broad white house on the Oyster River in Durham, where Sullivan divided his time between his farm and a thriving law practice.

They met several other horsemen on the way—men from Northwood, Deerfield, Nottingham, and Lee—all armed and also heading toward the Sullivan house. Caleb wondered at their boisterous good humor. Laughing, joking, everyone seemed charged with high spirits. There was a holiday exuberance about these men.

"The tension's broke, lad," the Captain said to Caleb, as they jogged side by side along a wide stretch of road. "Finally, at long last, there's to be some action."

They found the same holiday spirit when they pulled up before the Sullivan farmhouse in midmorning and tethered their mounts. Caleb estimated that there must be at least thirty men milling about the farmyard, talking and joking in small groups.

As Caleb and Captain McClary prepared to walk toward a knot of men a few yards away, Zeb hung back. Caleb looked at him inquiringly.

"My mount favors her left forefoot," Zeb said gruffly. "I'll join you after I look her over."

McClary strode to the horse and inspected its hoof. "I see nothing amiss."

"It could be a bruise," Zeb answered. "Let me check further."

McClary shrugged. "As you wish. You'll find me with Sullivan." Motioning Caleb to follow, he walked toward the group of men and asked for Major Sullivan.

The Major could be found at the riverbank, they were informed. As they walked on, McClary suddenly wheeled about. "Look ye there," he said grimly, pointing to a rider on a galloping horse heading down the road to Portsmouth.

"Zeb!" Caleb exclaimed.

McClary spat. "Aye, that's Zeb. His mount has made a quick recovery. I wondered what he had in mind. Now there's no question. Our bully boy's off to spread the alarm in Portsmouth."

Caleb's eyes opened wide. "Can we stop him?"

McClary shook his head. "It's not worth the effort. He'll find Wentworth's been alerted long before this. I'd say it's good riddance."

"But he has your horse!"

"I'll have my horse back, never fear," the Captain replied, "and he had best be unharmed."

"I've brought you nought but trouble," Caleb said miserably.

The Captain shook his head. "Not so. You've brought yourself, and I'm thankful for that. Ye remind me so much of your pa, it's almost like having young John Stark beside me again." He clapped Caleb on the shoulder. "We'll worry about Zeb when we reach Portsmouth. Now our task is to find Sullivan." He nodded toward the steep bank leading to the Oyster River. "Watch your footing. We can ill afford an injury at this point."

As the pair felt their way cautiously down the bank, they could see Sullivan and two other men closely inspecting a gundalow—the clumsy, flat-bottomed craft with leg-of-mutton sail that served as the workhorse of river shipping for the Piscataqua River area. Sullivan turned quickly at the sound of their approaching footsteps. Then his rugged features broke into a smile at the sight of McClary. "Andrew!" he exclaimed, striding toward them. In a moment, he was at their side, and the two men were shaking hands vigorously.

"You got the word, Andrew," Sullivan exclaimed, "and fast time ye made reaching here!"

McClary nodded his shaggy head. "Aye, John." He motioned Caleb to his side. "And I brought a young friend with me—John Stark's boy, Caleb."

Sullivan seemed sincerely pleased to meet Caleb. He held his hand in so tight a grip that Caleb thought he would break the bones. Caleb gave a sigh of relief as Sullivan released him.

"Now I'd like ye to meet two friends of mine," Sullivan said, leading the way toward the men who were standing beside the beached gundalow. "Paul, Eli," he said, "here's two new recruits."

As the men turned to face them, Caleb gave an involuntary gasp, which he immediately attempted to mask with a cough. For the man who stood nearer to him, his smooth round face fixed in a toothless grin, appeared to be totally devoid of hair. His scalp was pink and shiny. He had neither eyebrows nor eyelashes, a lack which focused attention on bright blue eyes that gazed upon the world with the curious, innocent look of a child. *He looks like a big, over-*

grown baby, Caleb thought, noting the man's squat, roly-poly body supported by bowed legs.

Half expecting a childish treble, Caleb blinked as the hairless man introduced himself in a rough, gravelly voice. "Eli Vanderhoff at yer service," he announced.

Caleb swallowed hard as he shook hands. "Caleb Stark," he said weakly.

"Eli's my best hand at the mill," Major Sullivan said.

Eli turned his toothless grin on McClary. "Works me like a dog, and pays a mere pittance. But I put up with it."

Sullivan winked at Caleb. "He puts up with me, for no one else will put up with *him*." He turned quickly to the man at his other side, a stocky man of swarthy complexion who stood quietly listening to the talk. "But here. I'm amiss in not introducing an honored guest—Paul Revere. This is the man who brought us the news from Boston."

Andrew McClary and Caleb quickly shook Revere's hand. "Heard tell of you," McClary said. "Ye must be done in for fair after such a ride."

Revere's dark eyes brightened momentarily, bringing a youthful look to his tired face. "It was not a pleasure trip," he admitted. "But from the looks of this assemblage, I'd say 'twas worth the effort."

"Ye did not waste your time," Sullivan assured him. "Ye know," he said to McClary, "this man slipped out of Boston yesterday—and how he did that, I'll never know, with Gage's troops demanding passes from every living being that tries to leave the town, but he did it, and I'll not ask him how."

Revere winked.

"No matter," Sullivan continued after a slight pause. He looked disappointed, Caleb thought, not to have gained more information. "The fact is, he did it—riding sixty miles over winter roads to Sam Cutts in Portsmouth."

"Your Sam Cutts is a youngish-appearing man," Revere

broke in. "Would that all heads of our Committees of Safety could be so youthful. 'Tis the young bloods are eager for action."

McClary frowned. "I'd not call myself young."

"No offense," Revere said hastily. "Such men as you are a boon to the cause. We need more Indian war veterans who are willing to help. But, with most of us, middle age and accumulating property make us more cautious."

"Aye," McClary agreed. "My trouble is, I've never learned caution."

Sullivan laughed. "No more have I." He gazed quizzically at Revere. "Nor you. I've heard often enough of bold Revere. Yet you, I dare say, can own to about forty years."

Revere smiled, white teeth flashing in his swarthy face. "You guess well. Some of us never do learn."

Eli looked morose. "I learn right enough. But it don't do me a spot of good. Wheresoever that hothead Major of mine goes, there also I must trail along."

"You know well enough, Eli," Sullivan said with mock seriousness, "if ever I tried to leave you beind, ye'd moon and mope the whole day through."

Eli drew himself up to full height, his round body teetering on bandy legs. "Not so," he sputtered. "By Godfrey, I keep tryin' to talk sense to ye, but ye don't listen. I needs must go along to protect ye from yourself."

"True," Sullivan agreed. "You're a good steadying influence." He turned to Revere. "Perhaps you have need of someone like Eli to curb your rashness, Paul. Then ye would think twice before riding as ye did yesterday." He turned to McClary. "Ye know, after he arrived at Sam Cutts' dwelling last evening, he tarried only long enough to eat a morsel. And then he needs be off again, to alert me in Durham. The man was near reeling when he dismounted."

"A moment's dizziness," Revere protested. "But it took little persuasion to have me stay the night."

Sullivan snorted. "Ye agreed only after I offered to send my own horsemen to spread the word."

"I needed the rest," Revere admitted, "and I thank you for it." He looked closely at Sullivan. "Are matters well in hand now?"

"As well as can be." Sullivan nodded toward the gundalow. "We have this boat in readiness, and two more we can use, if needed. Armed horsemen are assembled, anxious to be off. I'd say we're ready. My only regret is that I must temporarily stay behind."

McClary was puzzled. "You'll not join us, John?"

"Oh, yes," Sullivan assured him. "I'll be in Portsmouth, never fear. But for now I've been assigned a special task by the Committee of Safety. I can best fulfill my duty here."

Caleb was curious to know the nature of the Major's mysterious task. But it was obvious that Sullivan had said all he intended.

Revere seemed satisfied. "My work here's complete," he said. "I'll be off to Boston. Truth to tell, I'm that anxious to see my wife and newborn son again, I can't abide more delay."

McClary slapped his back. "A new father! Congratulations! How old is the lad?"

"Only a week," Revere answered quickly. "Rachel is doing well. Else I'd dare not have left her, even for this short time."

They walked up the bank toward the barn, where they found Revere's horse already saddled and looking none the worse for her long ride. She was a frisky little sorrel mare, fourteen hands high—a small horse, but the common size for a New Englander to be riding.

As Revere vaulted into the saddle, the mare skittered about, performing an impatient dance. Revere patted her neck. "She too is anxious to be off. Good-by, friends. Pay my respects to the King!" He wheeled his horse about and waved a hand in farewell.

They watched him off—the mare pacing sure-footed down the snowy road, and the man sitting his mount as if he and the horse were one. That was Caleb's last sight of Paul Revere, but the picture of the stocky man on the little horse was burned indelibly in his memory.

"Well, John," McClary said impatiently, "I also feel it's high time to be off. The day is wasting."

"My thoughts exactly," Sullivan agreed. "Will you accompany the party, Eli? Be my eyes and ears in Portsmouth, until I can journey there myself."

Eli looked disappointed. "If ye wish it so," he grumbled, "though I do hate to leave ye to look after yerself." Suddenly he fingered his bald head. "But I can't go this way! It's not fitting for me to visit town with my pate naked as a jaybird!"

Sullivan laughed. "Get your wig, then, and hurry."

As Eli scurried toward the farmhouse, Sullivan strode toward the group of armed men gathered in the yard. Many of them had noted the activity and were already in the saddle. "Give me your attention," Sullivan shouted. "I cannot accompany you to Portsmouth, much as I wish to. But I'll be with you soon as I can." He ignored the buzz of questions his statement produced and turned to McClary, who was already mounted. "Good luck, Captain. I'll see you in town."

As Caleb retrieved his musket and raced to his horse, Eli came running from the house. He held a musket in one hand and a small wheel of cheese in the other. On his head a ragged gray wig slipped over one eye in rakish fashion as he ran. With an oath, Eli snatched it off. As he reached his tethered horse, he thrust it into the saddlebag and threw the cheese on top of it. "Time enough to wear a wig when I reach town," he muttered.

Caleb and McClary exchanged glances. "By the time Eli reaches Portsmouth," the Captain said, "I fear he'll have a cheese full of hair."

Caleb began to laugh. "Or a wig full of cheese."

McClary's eyes opened wide at the thought and suddenly he too was laughing, a booming gust of mirth that seemed to come from deep in his paunch. Abruptly, his laughter ceased, as he observed Sullivan's growing impatience.

"Mount up!" Sullivan ordered.

Cheers were mixed with profanity, as some balky steeds fought the bit. And then they were off. Out the farmyard and down the road, a jingling, high-spirited procession, with steaming breath of men and horses mingling in the clear, cold air. Caleb felt the blood pumping fast through his veins. He was off to high adventure—to capture a royal fort, by mighty!

6

It was past the noon hour when Caleb and Captain Mc-Clary, a short distance in advance of their party, reached the prearranged rallying point of Stoodley's Tavern in Portsmouth. They found a hundred men crowding around the big, gambrel-roofed tavern on Daniel Street. Young and old, mostly in working clothes, they all had one thing in common: each man carried a weapon. There were heavy Brown Bess muskets of British manufacture, old Spanish fusees, a few unwieldy matchlocks, and antique French muskets dating back to the reduction of Louisburg.

As they dismounted and tethered their mounts to the hitching rail, McClary gave an exclamation of surprise. He walked quickly to a drooping gray mare hitched to the far end of the rail. "Here's my mare that Zeb took," he said, a note of concern in his voice. He ran expert hands over the tired creature. "She's been ridden hard," he said at length, "but seems in fair shape."

Caleb looked grim. "Better shape than Zeb will be, if I lay hands on him."

"Truth to tell, I wouldn't mind greeting that lad myself," McClary quietly admitted. "We'll keep our eyes peeled." He glanced up quickly as Eli rode toward them.

Eli slid off his horse and, after jumping up and down a few times to flex his legs, pushed his face up close to the graying muzzle of his horse. "You slab-footed bag of bones," he growled, "did ye think to jounce me to bits? I'm on to your tricks, never fear."

The old horse regarded Eli with gentle eyes and affectionately nuzzled him. Eli leaped back. "Think to bite me, do ye? By jingo, I'll tan your hide one of these days. You'd do well to remember that."

He dug into the capacious pocket of his great coat and drew out a piece of maple sugar, which he held flat in his hand beneath the horse's mouth. She chewed it quickly and thrust her neck forward to investigate Eli's pocket. "Don't be greedy," Eli grumbled, as he pushed her away. "I must bribe her with sweets, else she'll do me a mischief," he confided in a whisper to Caleb.

Caleb laughed. "She likes you, Eli."

The little man glowered. "That's all a show. I know the beast well. Beneath that sweet face, she's a horror."

McClary winked at Caleb. "Please, Eli," he said, pretending to be shocked. "That's no way to talk of your lady friend."

"Lady friend!" Eli shouted. "You know well I have no lady friend, Captain. I'm too smart for that."

"Excuse me," McClary said innocently. "I thought that was why you brought your wig to town—to impress the ladies."

Eli felt his bald head. "My wig! I clean forgot to wear

my wig!" Frantically he rummaged in his saddlebag and finally drew out the wig. He blinked, holding it at arm's length as he looked at it unbelievingly. "Did you ever see the likes of this?" he demanded.

Caleb never had. The jouncing ride had mixed cheese and wig, just as Captain McClary had predicted. The cheese-encrusted object that Eli now held in his hand resembled a drowned rat—and, Caleb thought as he wrinkled his nose, smelled just about as bad.

"A cheese wig!" McClary exclaimed. "You'll start a new fashion." He laughed until tears came to his eyes. His big hand slapped his knee breeches.

Eli stared round-eyed at the Captain for a moment, and then to Caleb's surprise he too began to laugh. With a flourish, he fixed the evil-smelling wig on his bald head.

"One thing I'll say," McClary gasped between spasms of laughter, "you're in no danger of scalping. No redskin would want such a trophy."

Eli jumped about, stamping his feet in imitation of a war dance. His tethered mare watched his antics with mild curiosity. Suddenly, as he came within range, she extended her neck and nipped the wig from his head.

With a bellow of rage, Eli turned and attempted to wrest it back. The mare threw back her head, there was a ripping sound, and the tattered wig lay in two sections on the trodden snow.

Eli shook his fist at the horse. "You limb of Satan! Is it cheese ye have a taste for? I'll ram this wig down your throat."

Caleb noted that McClary was becoming impatient. "Come, man," the Captain said. "Your horse did you a favor. I have a wig at home will fit ye as well and smell a bit sweeter."

Eli looked at him shrewdly. "Have ye now, Captain. A wig for me?"

McClary nodded. "And a hat to go with it. On condition I hear not one more word about that monstrosity."

"My lips are sealed," Eli assured him. "In return for the favor, Captain, would ye like me to look after your mount?"

"I'd be obliged," McClary replied. "I must get to the tavern and see Major Stoodley."

Caleb wasn't invited, but as McClary entered the packed tavern he trailed along behind and merged unnoticed in the crush of men who filled the big room. He didn't intend to miss any of this day's excitement. There was much loud conversation and excited laughter. Caleb had never before seen men worked up to such a pitch. No doubt the rum was doing its part, he thought; almost every man in the room was clutching a mug.

A cautious distance away from McClary, yet within earshot, he waited behind a post as the big man approached a beetle-browed individual who frowned at the boisterous men around him.

"Good day, Major Stoodley," McClary said amiably. "Your tavern does a rousing trade."

Stoodley nodded glumly. "It's a trade I'd gladly dispense with."

"Why, Major," McClary said innocently, "your tavern seems the most popular spot in town."

"Enough," Stoodley said roughly. "I'm in no mood to play games. This tavern's my livelihood." He nodded toward the stairs. "Up there's the best dance floor in town. The gentry gather here for their socials, and they pay well for the privilege. They'll not look kindly on this gathering."

McClary's eyes narrowed. "You trying to tell me we're not welcome here?"

Stoodley looked pained. "You know better than that, Andrew. It's just that I wish you'd picked another rally point." His glance flickered over the jostling crowd of armed men. "Look at 'em," he demanded. "This room's a tinderbox, ready for a spark to set off the whole business."

McClary grinned. "They seem jovial enough. I'd say the tinder in this room is pretty moist."

"A mob's a mob," Stoodley insisted. "You mind what happens with the Pope's Day parade in Boston. That starts out all frolic, too. But a few well-planted words can change that. It can end up with burning and bloodshed."

"These are all your friends, Major," Andrew McClary said soothingly. "Do you fear your friends?"

Stoodley looked at him darkly. "Separate and apart—each by his own—these are my friends. Together, they're a mob. And I fear the mob. I've seen too well the mischief a mob can do. It's a huge, brainless thing, working on naught but emotion, ready to be led this way and that by anyone who captures its fancy."

"Ye speak the truth," McClary soberly agreed. "Would it set your mind to rest if I vowed to help hold our friends in check, while in this tavern?"

"It would," Stoodley said instantly. "For I know they'll heed you—for good or ill."

"Then you have my word."

Stoodley relaxed a trifle. " 'Tis well." He winced as a long-legged youth suddenly leaped upon a nearby table and swung his broad-brimmed hat in wide circles. "We're going to take a glass of wine!" the youth shouted.

From all over the room came a booming response. "With Captain Cochran—Cocharine!"

Mugs banged on tables as the refrain grew in volume.

> "We're going to take a glass of wine,
> With Captain Cochran—Cocharine!"

Caleb, hearing it taken up by more voices outside the tavern, felt a vague disquiet. There seemed to be an ominous, threatening undercurrent in this massed chanting of an apparently meaningless rhyme.

McClary frowned. "What means this?"

The innkeeper raised his voice, in order to be heard over the din. Caleb inched closer. "A silly verse," Stoodley said sourly, "but it's caught their fancy. I'll tell ye the story when I can hear myself speak."

It was several minutes before the hubbub subsided enough for Stoodley to make himself heard in a normal tone of voice. Yesterday, he told them, the moment Tom Pickering had heard of Paul Revere's message, he had visited his good friend, Captain John Langdon, both men being leaders of the Portsmouth Sons of Liberty. After discussing the reported approach of British troops to seize the powder in Fort William and Mary, Pickering had casually suggested paying a visit to the fort's commander, Captain John Cochran. "Let's take a glass of wine with Captain Cochran," he had said to Langdon.

"Well," Stoodley continued, "you can imagine how that set with Langdon. He told the story on himself later. He admitted that for a moment he feared Pickering had gone daft. So he tried to calm him, saying, 'It won't do to make a social call, considering the present state of affairs.'

"Pickering told him then he wasn't planning on making a *social* call. 'With twenty or more men, we could make a most *unsocial* call at the fort,' he said."

Stoodley permitted himself a grim smile. "Then Langdon got the message. What Pickering proposed was that they storm the fort with twenty or more men—a sound-enough plan, for Cochran has only a token guard force. Langdon agreed to that soon enough. He'd gladly take such a glass of wine with Captain Cochran."

McClary grinned. " 'Tis a good rallying cry—and better for the efforts of the amateur versifier." He repeated it softly.

> "We're going to take a glass of wine,
> With Captain Cochran—Cocharine!"

Stoodley tilted his head. "Hark!" The group around him listened intently, trying to catch the sound that had alerted the Major. From a distance came the *rat-a-tat-tat* of a drum.

"Now it has begun," Stoodley said quietly. "They're beating Assembly."

In a moment the tavern noise was reduced to a muted undercurrent, as all ears became attuned to the distant drum.

The drubbing drew nearer—and now other drums were heard, seemingly converging from three directions. There was a loud whoop from the men in the tavern as, with a concerted rush, they jostled and pushed to reach the street.

"Plenty of room in here now for the gentry," McClary observed dryly.

"Praise be," said Stoodley. "There's to be more entertainment in Market Square than I can provide."

Slowly he walked with his friends out the tavern door as the last of his customers rushed to the street.

Caleb, a cautious distance behind, slipped unobtrusively into the crowd on Daniel Street. Now he could see the drummer, halfway up the street—a chunky lad with a wide grin, stepping high to the quick cadence of his drumbeat. *Rat-a-tat-tat!* In a blur of motion, the sticks beat a commanding rhythm on the scarred drumhead. "Come with me. Come with me," the drum seemed calling to Caleb.

The call must have been a compelling one, for just about every man on the street was falling in line behind the drummer. Caleb too joined the noisy, straggling procession, his moccosined feet making a rhythmic *splat-splat* in the thin layer of muddy snow churned by marching feet.

"Where ye been, lad?" Eli's familiar voice at his shoulder caused Caleb to turn his head. The pace was a quick one for Eli's short legs. Although the day was cool, Caleb saw beads of perspiration on his forehead, beneath the tricorne he had somehow obtained to shield his bald head. Eli was puffing, but his face bore a look of pure delight.

"Been looking for ye," Eli said. "Never do to miss the fun."

"I don't intend to," Caleb assured him. "Where we heading?"

Eli nodded toward an imposing building near the center of Market Square. "Town House. That's the gathering place. Look at 'em come!"

Armed men were streaming into the square from all directions—up from the waterfront, in from the Plain, down from Schoolhouse Hill. It was a colorful gathering, as the men clustered together in front of the Town House. Their loose greatcoats, flapping about stockinged calves, were as various in color as dyes taken from bark of the oak, sumach, and other trees could make them. As Caleb and Eli entered the broad square, two more contingents were being led in by drummers. The insistent *rat-a-tat-tat* throbbed in the clear air.

Eli peered closely toward the two-story Town House, and his face broke into a wide, toothless grin. "By jolley, I see him! There's Captain McClary on the steps." He nudged Caleb sharply in the ribs. "See him? See him?"

Caleb winced. "I see him," he said shortly. He quickly moved a step away, as Eli excitedly attempted to nudge him again.

"And look who's with him," Eli said, his voice rising. "Langdon and Pickering. All the leading citizens, ye might say. Oh, lad, this is what you might call an occasion."

"Good," Caleb said shortly, "but if we don't get closer, we'll not hear a word that's said."

Eli chuckled "I can tell ye what they'll say. 'To the fort!' they'll say. That's all. 'To the fort!' "

Caleb walked quickly toward the Town House as a conservatively dressed man in a plum-colored greatcoat, standing on the broad steps, help up his hands for silence.

"That's Captain Langdon," Eli said, as he followed Caleb.

A youngish man to have such a reputation, Caleb thought. He looked to be in his early thirties. The Captain's booming voice was lost in the general hubbub. But as Caleb and Eli pushed their way to a good vantage point near the steps, the crowd's babble diminished. Now they could plainly hear Langdon's voice, vibrant with emotion. "And who's to tell us we have no right to the powder in Fort William and Mary? It's the property of our province. That's our powder—as much as it is that of General Gage. Who's to tell us we can't claim what is our own—before it's seized by the lobsterbacks?"

The crowd cheered wildly. Langdon again raised his hands for silence.

"Hear me out. 'Twill take more than huzzas and halloos to get this powder." He paused and looked solemnly at the men clustered below him. "It means that every man here must put his life on the line. Are ye ready for such action?"

A deep roar came from the crowd, sending a shiver down Caleb's spine.

"We're with ye, Captain!" Eli shouted.

The cry instantly was taken up by men around them.

Caleb gulped. "How many soldiers at the fort?"

"A paltry force of invalids," Eli said contemptuously. "Cochran has but three regulars, and I understand today he's recruited two volunteers. Two foolish pups, still wet behind the ears. There'll be no more than six of 'em to meet us."

Caleb considered. "Six men with cannon can do a deal of mischief."

"Are ye fearful, lad?" Eli demanded.

"I don't think so," Caleb said slowly, as he honestly considered this charge. "Perhaps I have too much caution in me, but I don't think I'm fearful."

Eli looked at him steadily for a moment, and then his

face relaxed. "Just like your pa," he said. "John Stark's a great one to consider the odds, but no one doubts his courage. Nor do I doubt yours, lad." He swung about sharply, as several men in the crowd pointed toward the far end of Market Square.

"Chief Justice coming!" An excited babble arose as all heads turned toward a rapidly approaching high-wheeled carriage, drawn by a pair of bays, their breath steaming.

"He'll make a fine hostage!" shouted a young lad, waving a fusee of ancient manufacture.

Langdon glared down at him. "I'll have no violence here!" he roared. "Save yourself for the fort."

When the visibly worried driver reined in his horses near the Town House steps, Chief Justice Atkinson descended from the carriage. His thin, wrinkled face was fixed in a scowl. Imperiously he waved his silver-headed cane at the crowd that blocked his way to the steps.

There was a moment of indecision and mumbled imprecations before the men standing before him pushed back to form a small corridor through which he could walk. Head high, step firm, the old Chief Justice walked slowly through the threatening crowd, looking neither right nor left.

"A hard man," Eli observed. "I'd hate to be brought before him."

"He seems a brave man," Caleb observed truthfully, wondering how he himself would act if he had to take this stroll through a hostile mob. A vision of his own father as a youth walking through two lines of jeering savages flashed through his mind. For the first time he truly felt the degree of courage his father had displayed on that long-ago day.

He felt an unwilling respect for Atkinson, who obviously had dressed for this occasion as carefully as he would for an appointment with the Royal Governor. His three-cornered hat was set precisely atop his powdered hair, which was gathered in a queue at the back and tied with a bow of black ribbon. His side locks were frizzled and powdered. An expanse of starched ruff showed at neck and wrist, partially covered by a well-fitting waistcoast of rich maroon. His long stockings and tight knee breeches were immaculate. As he mounted the steps of the Town House to take his place beside the Committee of Safety gathered there, sunlight glinted on his large silver shoe buckles.

The Chief Justice nodded a perfunctory greeting to the men beside him on the steps. He then turned his full attention to the crowd below. His dark eyes flashed defiance. A hush fell over the assembly, as in his crisp, dry voice he told his audience that he was here in his official capacity as Chief Justice of the Province and Governor Wentworth's deputy. "It has been cried about the town that you are here gathered to attack and forcibly enter His Majesty's Castle of Fort William and Mary. In the name of His Excellency, Governor John Wentworth, I bid you disperse and return peaceably to your homes." He paused, looking piercingly from face to face, as if he would commit each to memory.

There was a moment's silence, as the crowd stared uneasily back at him and looked for direction to the stolid faces of the Committee members on the steps.

The hush was broken by a deep, drawling voice from the center of the crowd. "Git home yerself, Atkinson, lest ye land in trouble!"

Atkinson's moment of authority was over, Caleb could see, as a great shout of mirth burst from the crowd, interspersed with ribald suggestions directed at the Chief Justice.

Langdon held up his hand for silence, but there was no holding the crowd now.

"To the fort!" someone cried. The echoed phrase spread to the outermost reaches of the crowd. "To the fort! To the fort!" It became a chant, a demanding, threatening rhythm that would not be thwarted.

Caleb saw the Committee members on the steps confer briefly. Then, with an apologetic shrug to Atkinson, Langdon rushed down the stairs into the crowd, followed by McClary and Pickering. There was a great roar as they were engulfed in the throng, which now numbered almost three hundred.

As if following a prearranged plan, although Caleb had heard no orders given, the armed men turned away from the Town House and moved down Pleasant Street toward the waterfront in a long, straggling column.

"Come on!" Eli shouted to Caleb. "You want to get left?" His bandy legs moved with amazing speed. Caleb lengthened his own stride to keep up. At the end of the square, he allowed himself one backward glance toward the Town House steps. The lone figure of Justice Atkinson still stood there, leaning on his cane, gazing at the departing crowd. His coach waited for him, the horses pawing the ground.

Caleb felt a sudden stab of sympathy for the old man. He's doing his duty as he sees it, he thought.

"Hurry," Eli prodded. Caleb noticed he was dropping behind. Better not to think at a time like this. Concentrate on what's at hand. From all about him the insistent cry beat on his ears: "To the fort!"

7
☆ ☆
☆

Caleb felt a twinge of conscience as he was jostled forward on the dock. If Captain McClary were to see him now he would forbid him to take any further part in this dangerous enterprise. He had been allowed to come to Portsmouth only to act as an observer for John Stark.

But McClary was nowhere in sight, and it was too late to turn back. There was no denying the pressure of the crowd, pushing toward dockside. He was near the edge of the dock now, and a few feet below him two gundalows, with sails furled, strained at ropes which held them tight to the pilings. They resembled flat-bottomed scows bearing stubby masts. As men just ahead of Caleb prepared to jump into them, helping hands were extended by those already standing in the boats. One of the sturdy craft, which ordinarily carried cargoes weighing between thirty and forty tons, was filled with armed men. It cast off, as Caleb watched, and moved slowly out into the cove. There was a cheer as the leg-of-mutton sail was raised and caught an offshore breeze. Ponderously the loaded craft headed toward Point-of-Graves.

Soon it would be Caleb's turn to jump into the remaining gundalow. There were only a few men ahead of him. His heart beat fast and his mouth felt dry. At the pressure of a hand on his arm, he turned his head quickly to find Eli at his elbow. Eli's toothless grin was a strangely comforting sight, assuring him that he was not a lone stranger in this throng.

" 'Twon't do to lose each other," Eli's voice rasped in his ear. "Look sharp now," he admonished, as Caleb was pushed to the very edge of the dock.

Caleb grasped a hand outstretched by a man in the gundalow. He jumped into the boat and found his footing as Eli leaped down beside him.

A morose-looking individual standing beside Caleb shivered as the cool sea breeze ruffled his hair. "We'll all expire of the pleurisy 'fore we reach the fort," he predicted.

A chunky young fellow crowded against Caleb amended this. "If the cannon don't get us first," he said in a surprisingly cheerful tone.

Caleb gulped. The words brought home the fact that he was committed to a dangerous mission. No boyish prank, this. He was engaged in men's work now.

Eli's voice was gruff. "What's the odds? Ye want to live forever?"

The morose passenger gave him a baleful glance. "I wouldn't mind. How do ye go about it?"

"I wouldn't know," Eli retorted. "As for me, I plan a short life and a merry one."

"Cast off!" The order from dockside forestalled further observations by Eli, who immediately turned his attention to the mooring line.

In a matter of minutes, sail was set and the loaded craft moved sluggishly out.

Slowly the two gundalows, each filled with about one hundred men, sailed through the swirling green water of the cove. At the north side of Point-of-Graves, they were joined by a motley collection of small craft—wherries, whaleboats, canoes—which swung in behind the gundalows. Looking at the bobbing flotilla strung out in the wake of his boat, Caleb estimated that there must be at least one hundred and fifty men gathered in these small boats. They would make a sizable assault force.

After passing the point, the rushing tide took hold of the boats—through the Narrows between Governor's Island and Peavey's Island, past Pull-and-Be-Damned, past Pest House Inlet. They were nearing their goal now, sailing near a cluster of houses on the Newcastle shore of Great Island, straight toward the high eight-sided lighthouse at the tip of Castle Point.

There, rising from the sea, was an outcropping of rock with steeply slanting cliffs that resembled the back of a gigantic whale. Perched atop this rocky formation was the squat, forbidding outline of Fort William and Mary. The British flag on a tall pole snapped in the breeze, its bright red and blue giving a touch of color to the otherwise drab scene. Foam-flecked waves lapped the cliff's rocky base. Gulls screamed as they wheeled and dived. But Caleb could see no sign of human activity about the fort.

Perhaps the soldiers have left, he thought, and drew a surprising sense of relief from this surmise. The thought was short-lived, as the scrape of metal on stone drew his attention to the parapet. His eyes opened wide as, at the top of masonry walls surrounding the fort, he saw the mouths of three cannon trained on the boats.

Eli also was looking closely at the cannon mouths. "See what's been wheeled up to affright us," Eli said softly. "Four-pounders, by the look of 'em."

"They'll smash this scow to kindling," the morose passenger volunteered.

"Never fear," Eli said kindly. "If a ball comes close, I'll whack it aside 'fore it upsets ye."

"Whack it with your head," the man replied. "That's hard enough."

"I'd like to bump heads with you, mister," Eli growled. "If only—"

His sentiments remained half expressed, as the leading gundalow suddenly swung about while still thirty yards away from the cliff. The smaller boats followed suit. As their gundalow heeled about, Caleb's chunky neighbor grasped him for support. "We'll all end up in the drink together," the chunky one observed, still in a cheerful voice.

"Hush," Eli commanded. He was watching a tall figure in the first gundalow. The man stood facing the fort and was evidently about to shout a message through cupped hands. "It's Pickering," Eli said. "Hark now!"

"Hark yourself," the glum one muttered. "You're the one does all the jabbering."

Eli ignored him, as Pickering's voice carried faintly across the water.

"Halloo-o-o there!" Pickering shouted toward the fort.

There was silence. After a moment's pause, Pickering shouted again.

"Halloo-o-o there! We call upon you to surrender!"

This time there was an unmistakable response—a tremendous clap of sound, bright flashes of fire, and puffs of black smoke, as the three cannon opened fire. Caleb involuntarily ducked as a geyser of water exploded to the left of the boat. Two more waterspouts—one behind and another to the right of the gundalows—marked the spots where the other two cannon balls fell harmlessly into the sea.

Waving his musket above his head, Pickering leaped from the lead boat and churned forward through knee-deep water, heading for the cliff. With a great shout, the others in his boat jumped into the water. Widely spaced, in no apparent order, the men waded toward shore.

There was furious activity in Caleb's boat as it also drew near the reef that had stopped Pickering's craft.

"Looks like we'll get our boots wet this trip," Eli observed. Caleb's gaze was drawn once more to the high parapet where the cannon were still trained out to sea. He knew that their boat now was within easy range. His stomach tensed, waiting for the cannon to roar again.

"Are they waiting for us to come closer still?" Caleb asked.

"Dunno," Eli answered honestly. "Could be. But don't it cause ye to wonder that not one of their balls hit a ship? They're not that bad shots—not when we're in full view below 'em, like sitting ducks."

The morose one blinked. "You think they don't want to hit us?"

Eli shrugged. "If I was in the place of those few lads in the fort and saw a couple hundred men come storming toward me, I'd not want to get 'em too riled."

"You mean they'll put up nought but a token defense?" Caleb's chunky neighbor asked.

"I'll not say aye nor nay," Eli replied. "But it's a thought."

As their boat dropped anchor off the reef and his fellow passengers began jumping into the shallow water, Caleb hoped that Eli's guess was right. Although their boats were certainly easy targets now, not another shot had been fired from the fort.

With a grunt, Eli lowered himself into the water. Caleb splashed down beside him. "Over a bit," Eli ordered. "We don't want one lucky shot to do us both in."

Knee deep in icy sea water, Caleb involuntarily gasped as he walked forward. The cold water sent chills through his body, and soon both his legs felt frozen to the marrow. After a few steps, however, a blessed numbness set in, and Caleb found that he could endure the cold.

As they approached the high sloping cliff, he saw that the men from Pickering's crew were climbing with difficulty a steep, winding path that led up to the fort. As Caleb watched, a volley of musket fire came from the fort. At the first crack, the climbers threw themselves to the ground. Several fired futile shots at the high parapet. Their fire was not returned. In a few moments the men rose cautiously to their feet, and the slow march to the heights began again.

Caleb and Eli were now at the water's edge, picking their way gingerly over round, wet stones. Finally reaching a stretch of pebbled beach at the cliff's base, Caleb paused to chafe his numb legs. Slowly, feeling returned—but with it came agonizing pinpricks of pain. Eli too must have experienced the same sensation, for he winced as he stamped his bandy legs to restore their circulation.

"Let's move on," Eli said shortly. " 'Twon't do to let our muscles knot up."

The cliff seemed much steeper to Caleb now that he was at the bottom, looking up at its rocky surface, partially covered with a thin layer of soil in which a few twisted trees had taken root. The narrow path, winding up between craggy outcroppings of rock, was wet and slippery with melting snow. But Caleb saw that at least fifty men were strung out along its winding length. The leaders were half-way to the summit and moving steadily forward.

Caleb took a deep breath and started up the path in advance of Eli. He held his musket in one hand, ready for instant action. With his free hand, he clutched any projection that would help speed his ascent. He was moving forward steadily now, concentrating on his footing. Behind him he could hear Eli, grunting and muttering.

Midway up the path, climbing became easier, as the cliff sloped toward the summit. At this point Caleb became intimately acquainted with a moss-covered boulder rimmed with snow. He threw himself headlong behind this rock as the unmistakable sound of small-arms fire came from the fort and lead pellets sang overhead, snipping twigs from a pine that clung to the cliff a few yards ahead of him.

Caleb pressed himself close to the cold earth. His heart beat fast. He felt hair prickle at the base of his scalp. So this was how it was! He had wondered earlier in the day how he would react if he found himself under direct musket fire. But then it had been an abstract question, as if he had been standing off to the side, observing a stranger. He had not thought that he would panic. Past events had proved to Caleb that he was as courageous as any of his friends.

But now, at this moment, finding himself actually under fire, Caleb knew that he was afraid. The deadly shot singing overhead was such an impersonal danger. A musket didn't care who or what it hit. With stinging finality, it could remove an eye or penetrate a brain.

A tremor ran through Caleb's limbs. Instantly he felt the reassuring pressure of a hand on his leg. Cautiously raising his head, he looked behind him. Eli, lying just below, gave a prodigious wink.

"We've found a cold bed," Eli said hoarsely.

Caleb gulped. "But a warm welcome." He noted that his voice sounded a bit shaky.

"No need to worry," Eli said promptly. "Those shots were meant more to dislodge birds from trees than to stop an assault. It's as I said, theirs is but a token defense."

As those above them on the path rose cautiously and continued on, Eli urged him forward. Crouching low and glancing repeatedly toward the top of the cliff, they continued their slow ascent. Caleb could see nothing of the fort they were approaching except the large British flag atop its high pole, stirring in the breeze. But suddenly, as they scrambled over a high outcropping of rock, Caleb realized they had attained the heights. Ahead of him, only a few rods away, he had his first close-up view of the fort—a grim stone structure consisting of a two-story building and several smaller ones, surrounded by ten-foot walls. It was set in the middle of a boulder-strewn field, where some brown clumps of grass and denuded trees were partially covered with a sprinkling of snow.

Eli nudged him. "This way," he whispered, as he took the lead, circling far to the left of the fort toward a clump of trees.

There must be some plan, Caleb thought, as he ran behind Eli. The men who had ascended the path ahead of him were fanning out, as if preparing to circle the fort. Except for the sound of running feet and a few low-voiced commands, there was an unnatural silence on this exposed hilltop. Though the sun shone brightly, Caleb had the same uneasy feeling he sometimes had in advance of a gathering storm. He glanced warily toward the ramparts, expecting musket shots at any moment. But all remained quiet.

As they reached a spot twenty yards from the western

wall of the fortification, Eli clutched Caleb's sleeve, pulling him to his knees behind a snow-drifted hummock.

"We're to attack on all quarters," Eli said. "I figure this wall's the easiest to scale."

Caleb looked dubiously at the high stonework, wishing that he could share Eli's optimism. Although apprehensive, he felt a rising sense of excitement as he watched a steady flow of men form a semicircle a discreet distance from the fort. They crouched behind every stone and tree large enough to offer protection. Muskets at the ready, they waited, tense and silent.

His fingers stiff with cold, Caleb primed his musket and put it on halfcock. "When do we pay our visit to Captain Cochran?" he whispered to Eli.

"When we're invited," Eli innocently replied. "It's not good manners to go where we're not invited."

On their extreme left, a tall man who must be Pickering leaped to his feet. "Charge!" he shouted. He rushed forward, discharging his musket as he ran. Instantly the field was swarming with men leaping from their places of concealment. Running forward, they converged on the fort. Their musket balls rattled against the stone walls like deadly hail.

"There's our invite!" Eli shouted. "Stick close."

As they ran forward, Caleb suddenly was conscious of return fire from the fort. Once again he heard shot whining overhead. But this time, so intent was he on gaining the wall, he gave it scarcely a thought.

Now he was almost there. He looked up, half expecting to see a musket muzzle pointing at him. Instead, he saw several members of the assault party who had scaled the redoubt and were now lying along its top, helping those about to climb the wall.

Caleb, leaping for one of the extended hands, found that he missed contact by a good two feet. Before he could try again, he was boosted into the air by a hand placed under his foot. As he flexed his knees and stretched upward again, the hand beneath his foot thrust upward with amazing strength.

"Up ye go," he heard Eli shout, and he popped upward like a jack-in-the-box and caught hold of the waiting hand. He swung for a moment, until his moccasined feet found a cranny in the wall to give him needed support. Another boost from below and a second helping hand from the wall enabled him to scramble up. It was a difficult climb, for he had to hold onto his precious musket.

Caleb was breathing hard as he paused on top of the wall and glanced into the inner courtyard. It seemed a long way down. But there was no time to dawdle. He dropped onto the snow-covered sod of the courtyard. He rolled over once after hitting the ground with a tingling shock that seemed to jar every bone in his body. His musket skittered away. As he frantically crawled to retrieve it, Eli landed beside him and rolled forward. Eli's musket and three-cornered hat went flying in opposite directions.

"Hells bells and panther tracks," Eli muttered, as he retrieved hat and musket. "Ye'd think they'd open the gate and let us in the easy way." He set the hat firmly on his bald head and closely inspected his musket.

Caleb, busily cleaning the snow from his own weapon, nodded in agreement. "You'd think so. I've yet to see a soldier here."

"We heard their cannon and muskets, though," Eli said, "loud and clear. They're about, never fear."

Caleb managed a grin. "You made a verse, Eli."

The bald one snorted. "There's scant time for versifying. Are ye all right, lad?"

"I trust so," Caleb said, as he gingerly arose. "Are you?"

Eli hoisted himself from the ground and flexed his bowed legs. "Good as ever—which ain't saying much."

A cheer drew their attention to a boisterous group gathered around a tall flagpole in the center of the courtyard.

They looked just in time to see the British flag being lowered unceremoniously to the ground.

"There it goes!" Eli shouted. "So much for the King!" He started toward the flagpole and then changed direction as men ran past them, heading toward a solidly constructed stone building at the north end of the courtyard. "Come on," he urged Caleb. "Let's see where our friends are heading." He started after them at a brisk clip. "Follow me, and ye'll stay out of trouble."

Caleb walked a few steps behind. "Seems to me that every place I follow you, I land spang in the *midst* of trouble."

Eli grunted and increased his pace. The interval between them lengthened. As Caleb began to double time, he was stopped abruptly in mid-stride by a hand that grasped his buckskin jacket and pulled him roughly backward behind a large barrel. Caught off balance, Caleb struggled to regain his footing. At the same time, he twisted about, straining to see whoever it was that detained him.

He gasped sharply as he found himself eye to eye with Zeb.

"Don't you make a fuss," Zeb said softly. Although the words were a command, there was a pleading note in Zeb's voice that made Caleb slowly lower his musket, which he was about to use as a club. "Please," Zeb continued hurriedly. "I need your help."

Caleb found it difficult to believe that this was the same boy he had last seen at the Sullivan farm. Zeb asking for help? Impossible. Yet there was no mistaking the entreaty in his words. Caleb allowed himself to be drawn down behind the barrel, as Zeb hunkered down beside him.

"I'm in deep trouble," Zeb said hoarsely.

Caleb agreed with him. "What are you doing here?" he demanded.

Zeb took a deep breath. "I'm helpin' defend this sad

excuse for a fort," he said. Then the story came in a rush of words. He told how he had set out from the Sullivan farm to warn the Governor in Portsmouth that a force was on the way to invade the fort. "A scurvy trick, ye may think," he acknowledged in a defensive tone, "but right according to my way of thinking."

"At least it rings of truth," Caleb acknowledged. "You've not made up some cock-and-bull fancy."

Zeb's shoulders drooped. So dejected did he look that Caleb felt a stirring of sympathy. "No use to lie now," Zeb said. "My lot can't be worse. And I thought myself so great, bringing the news to the Governor. He knew, of course. Everybody knew. I never did get to see the Governor. But I was brought to see Captain Cochran, just preparing to leave the Governor's house. 'A fine lad,' Cochran says to me. 'A bright lad. Your sentiments do ye honor. And how would ye like the privilege of defending the King's fort?' " Zeb looked beseechingly at Caleb. "What could I say? He took it for granted I was of age to bear arms, and I'd gone this far. How could I refuse him?"

Caleb looked incredulous. "Didn't ye know they'd drummed about town all day, asking for defenders, and none answered the call?"

"I did not," Zeb said miserably. "I was innocent as a babe."

Caleb struggled to hide a smile. Deliver him from such a babe as this. Aloud he said, "How many men does Cochran have here?"

"Only four besides myself," Zeb said scornfully, "and a mangy lot they are." His voice rose. "How was I to know the King's fort would be so ill manned? I expected a full company."

Thinking it was fortunate that Zeb's hopes were doomed, Caleb said, "In truth you didn't put up too great a defense."

"A token defense," Zeb burst out. "Nought but a token. That was the way Cochran would have it. Something to write in his report, but no blood spilled."

Caleb nodded. "We thought as much. And now that we're here, what's to become of you?"

"Ye must help me," Zeb implored. "Take me away with you."

Caleb marveled at Zeb's audacity. "As a prisoner, ye mean?" he asked innocently.

Zeb shook his head. "As a member of your party. I'm still in buckskin. None will question me if I board the gundalow with you."

"You ask a lot of me," Caleb said sternly. "Has your love for the Crown cooled so fast?"

"Grant me this one favor," Zeb pleaded. "I'll not be ungrateful."

Caleb regarded him silently for a long moment. It would be uncomfortable, he thought, returning home without Zeb and facing a barrage of questions from the Snavelys. And what of his pa? What would John Stark have him do in this instance? Should he leave an unwilling recruit for the British, or snatch him away? The longer he thought, the more certain he was as to what John Stark's answer would be. "I think Pa would have me help you," he said at length.

Zeb brightened. "Ye'll help?"

"Aye." Caleb's voice was flat. He didn't like this course of action, but he could think of no other. "My hand on it."

Zeb grasped his hand eagerly.

"You'd best make yourself scarce till it's time to leave," Caleb ordered.

"I'll lie low," Zeb assured him. "I know just the spot."

Trust Zeb to look ahead, Caleb thought. "Good," he said shortly. "I'll do what I can. But I make no promises."

"I expect none," Zeb said abjectly. "Whatever befalls, I've only myself to blame."

"You'll have me in tears," Caleb said sourly, "if I don't gag first. Now be off. I've work to do."

8

Caleb watched Zeb disappear into the hurrying crowd, and then, losing sight of him, he hurried toward the squat brick building which seemed to be the focal point of activity. It evidently was the powder house, judging by the number of barrels that were being carefully carried from its interior.

He had almost reached the building's open double doors when he caught sight of Captain McClary directing operations just outside the building. Quickly Caleb edged away. Here was the one person in all this company he definitely did not want to meet, for he knew that the Captain desired him to take no part in this operation.

Caleb walked quickly to the nearest refuge, a large stone building to his right. From the size of it, he presumed that this was the fort's headquarters and barracks. Now, however, it seemed comparatively deserted, as the main force of invaders clustered about the powder house.

Caleb cautiously pushed open the heavy entrance door and stepped inside. His nose wrinkled as he inhaled odors that over the years had become a tangible part of the building. Unwashed bodies, tobacco smoke, liquor fumes, discarded food scraps—all these lingering smells fused to create an overwhelming odor of stagnation.

As he stood quiet, fighting a rising wave of nausea, he heard in the next room a voice taut with emotion. "You've taken the fort. What more do you want of me?"

Walking softly, Caleb peered around the casement of an open door leading into a small guardroom. There, dimly visible in moted shafts of sunlight that shone through a barred window, Caleb saw three of the invaders facing a small man in British uniform. One tall figure he recognized as Captain Pickering.

"You've played a prudent role, Captain Cochran," he heard Pickering say. "I have no desire to humiliate you."

The little man pulled himself to his full height. "What can you do to humiliate me further?" Cochran demanded, his voice rising. He leaned toward Pickering, his red uniform coat almost touching Pickering's homespun jacket. "You've overrun my fort, made prisoners of my men."

Caleb smiled as he thought of Zeb. "*Almost* all are prisoners," he said to himself.

"Here, sir, is my sword," Cochran said stiffly, as he unsheathed his dress sword. "So that your victory may be complete."

Pickering raised his hand in protest. "Nay, Captain. Keep your side arms." He glanced about at his party of three, who stood impatiently watching this byplay. "Now, if you'll excuse us, I think we're needed at the powder house."

His men required no further invitation. As they charged out of the room past his place of concealment, Caleb shrank back farther into the shadows. Pickering followed, at a more leisurely pace, with Cochran a few steps behind him, the rejected sword still in his hand.

Without looking back, Pickering said soothingly, "We'll not trouble you much longer, Captain. Have patience."

Caleb noticed that this simple statement made Cochran fairly quiver with rage. His face flushed a mottled red hue and he raised his sword, as Caleb watched in alarm. "Patience!" he cried. "Patience! To stand idly by and watch my fort ransacked—" The thought was more than he could bear. With a strangled cry, he lunged toward Pickering, who wheeled about with one arm extended to shield himself from the expected blow.

The sword never found its mark, for Caleb leaped forward the moment Cochran attacked. Caleb's shoulder smashed against the officer's chest, throwing him backward. The shock of impact sent his sword flying from his hand. It clanged upon the stone floor, just out of reach, as Cochran and Caleb fell together and rolled about the floor, locked in combat.

The next moment Pickering was leaning over them. His face was grim and his grasp brutally strong as he clutched Cochran's neckpiece. The cocky little man seemed to bounce as Pickering drew him roughly to his feet.

"You villainous jackal," Pickering growled, still keeping tight hold on the officer. "Stab me in the back, would ye?" He shook the Captain to emphasize his words.

Cochran glared back. "You deserve no better."

Caleb, rising slowly to his feet, looked about him and recovered his musket, which he had left propped against the wall. He was preparing to leave as quietly as possible when his action was forestalled by a lantern-jawed member of Pickering's party, who had returned to discover what was delaying his chief.

Pickering thrust the Captain toward the lantern-jawed one. "Take him and tie him up with the others," he ordered.

As Cochran was prodded on his way out the door by Pickering's man, who obviously enjoyed this task, Pickering turned to Caleb. "Do I know you, lad?"

Caleb gulped. No way out now. By the look of him, this man would surely catch him in a lie. Tell the truth and take the consequences, Caleb decided. If only he could have kept out of sight. "I'm Stark, sir. Caleb Stark."

A quick smile lit Pickering's face. "You're the boy Mc-Clary mentioned to me. He's lost sight of you, and it worries him. He means to take good care of John Stark's boy."

"I shouldn't be here," Caleb blurted out. "It's not his fault. I came on an impulse."

"I'm glad that you're here, Caleb," Pickering told him gravely. "If you weren't, I might now be a dead man. I'm in your debt, and that's a fact."

"No need to feel a debt," Caleb protested, "but I would be thankful were you to say naught of my being here."

Pickering winked. "Mum's the word. It's the least I can do. Will ye accompany me to the powder house?"

Caleb looked doubtful. "I'd as soon not chance it. If I met Captain McClary there, he'd not look kindly on me."

"As you will," Pickering agreed. "But you still can help —if ye don't mind wet feet. There's need for many hands to carry powder barrels aboard the gundalows."

Caleb wondered afterward if he had been in his right mind when he'd volunteered for the task of carrying the barrels. It was exhausting work. Although his muscles were hardened by farm labor, his back and shoulders soon were aching from the heavy weight he carried. He was one of a file of men sloshing through knee-deep water from the shore to the two gundalows anchored thirty yards out, beyond the reef. Each man shouldered a barrel containing one hundred pounds of powder. Ninety-eight of these barrels were being passed from hand to hand down the precipitous path to the shore line.

Caleb made eight round trips from shore to gundalows before the last barrel was stowed on board. His task completed, he slumped wearily on a rock at the cliff's base.

Must be we've taken all we intend to this trip, he thought, as he watched the men who had been passing the barrels begin to clamber down the path. Slanting rays of a late-afternoon sun showed in sharp relief the lines in their drawn faces. This was not the boisterous group that had charged up the path to capture the King's fort. Here was a chilled, bone-tired company that had compressed a day's work into two short hours.

Now the rest of the company was beginning to swarm down the cliff, some taking a longer, circuitous path they had discovered. The beach was becoming crowded. Caleb looked with envy at these later arrivals, who didn't seem nearly as exhausted as those who had been passing the barrels.

Some men already were starting to wade out to the boats. In a moment, Caleb told himself, he would join them. But now he would enjoy the luxury of this cold rock seat. It seemed so good just to sit, though he was chilled and wet to the waist. For a moment his eyelids drooped.

"Caleb."

The sound of his name, whispered in his ear, caused him to sit bolt upright. Zeb's anxious face was close to his own.

"I'm here," Zeb said—quite unnecessarily, Caleb thought.

Caleb's tone was sour. "So I see." He rose stiffly to his feet. "We'd best get to the boat."

"Caleb!" Again he heard his name called. No mistaking the voice at his back that was now shouting to him. He turned to face Captain McClary.

"I thought I'd lost ye, lad. Where'd ye get to? I was that—" McClary's voice ended in a grunt, as he caught sight of Zeb. He leveled an accusing finger at the boy. "You! How dare ye show your face here?" His hand shot out and grasped Zeb's jacket in a tight grip. He pulled the boy toward him.

Zeb twisted impotently, attempting to break the strong grip. "Help me, Caleb," Zeb pleaded. "You promised."

McClary tightened his grip on the wriggling captive, as he turned an unbelieving gaze on Caleb. "You mean to help this peeled-heeled spawn of Satan?"

"I promised," Caleb admitted. He felt like sinking into the ground as he saw Captain Langdon and Eli push their way through a growing ring of onlookers. The strain of this afternoon's work was clearly visible on Eli's face, but he brightened when he saw Caleb. As his gaze swept over Zeb, his features tightened again. "Who's this?"

"This is Zeb," Caleb said in a low voice.

Eli's eyes widened. "By hokey! Ye caught him! Good work, lad!"

"I dunno if it's good work or not," McClary said shortly, as he released his hold on Zeb. "You can speak to Caleb about that."

Langdon frowned. "What does that mean?"

Caleb straightened his shoulders, but, surprisingly, before words would come, Zeb spoke up. "It means nought," he said in a low voice. "I've caused trouble enough. You have me now. So let that be an end to it."

Caleb looked at the boy with new respect. In this moment of crisis, Zeb had regained his spirit. There was defiance now in Zeb's gaze, and a firm set to his jaw.

"Is that the way you'd like it, Caleb?" McClary asked gravely.

"I'm sick at heart about this whole affair," Caleb said. He took a deep breath. "But truth is truth. And the simple truth is that I promised to help Zeb escape."

There was a sudden quiet as the circle of onlookers regarded him curiously. Caleb had the feeling that he was a bug pinned for exhibit.

Finally Langdon said in an unbelieving voice, "You promised that? Don't ye know it's been reported that your friend has sided with the King's men? That he helped defend the fort? Are you too of a similar mind?"

"I am not," Caleb answered promptly, "though you may find that hard to believe. I'd find it so myself, in your place." He looked closely at the faces surrounding him. Langdon and McClary's expressions were hard. Only in

Eli's face did he glimpse compassion. An ugly muttered undercurrent swept through the crowd. He caught the words "turncoat" and "royal lackey" directed at him.

"I do find it hard to believe," Langdon said shortly. "Can you give me one good reason why this royalist shouldn't be left here with his fellows?"

"You can't leave me," Zeb burst out. "I must get home."

"I should think ye'd like to stay here," McClary said innocently. "I have no doubt there'll be a court of inquiry when the British troops arrive, and then you can tell your story. Isn't that what you intended?"

"They don't trust me," Zeb said in a low voice. "I'll be kept under guard. I well may be pressed into service aboard their ship."

Langdon was becoming impatient. "Those thoughts are a bit late." He turned to Caleb. "Your friend stays behind," he said with finality. "As for you—"

"As for him, I'll vouch for his loyalty and courage," Pickering's crisp voice interrupted, as the tall captain pushed his way to their side.

Langdon's eyes narrowed. "Say ye so? Have ye proof?"

"I'm alive," Pickering answered simply. "I'd call that living proof." He put a protective hand on Caleb's shoulder. "This lad risked his life to save mine."

McClary looked abashed. "I didn't realize—" Impulsively he extended his hand, which Caleb grasped. "Forgive me, boy."

Langdon scratched his head. "But why does he insist on protecting this King-lover?"

"I don't know," Pickering answered promptly, "but if this lad befriended Old Scratch himself, I'd not question him."

"Amen," said Eli piously. He whacked Caleb on the back, causing him to bend forward like a willow in a high wind. "I'm with ye, lad."

There were shouts of encouragement from the crowd,

indicating to Langdon that its mood had changed. "So be it," he said shortly. "Let's have no more delay. To the boats —all of you." His glance, flickering over Zeb's face, included him in this general order.

Caleb noted Zeb's look of relief. "Watch your manners," he said in a quiet aside. "Don't forget I'm being held to account for you."

"I'll make certain sure he has good manners," Eli said gruffly. He motioned Zeb forward. "Go ahead of me to the boat. We'll be right behind. And hurry, or the only space left will be atop the mast."

Captain Langdon strode past them along the narrow beach. "Remove your shoes before boarding," he called. "Pass the word."

"Remove yer shoes," Eli bellowed. Caleb heard the cry repeated up and down the beach. All about him men were sitting to take off their footwear.

"Why concern ourselves with shoes?" Caleb asked.

With a mighty yank, Eli removed his second shoe. Kneading his feet to restore circulation, he did not bother to look up as he said, "The reason's plain as Bessie's bonnet. Once in that gundalow, we'll be settin' on gunpowder —barrels and barrels of gunpowder. One spark from a boot nail, and it's boom, bang, and away. Ye'll sail through the air—in assorted pieces."

It was a slow trip back to the Portsmouth docks. Both gundalows carried a heavy cargo of powder. Men sat where they could on top of the barrels. They were comparatively quiet now. Faces red from the cold, shoes tied about their necks; some shivering, others seized with fits of coughing— all uneasily conscious of the murderous cargo they carried.

Caleb somehow, without consciously thinking about it, felt older than he had earlier in the day, when he had set out with a light heart, looking forward to high adventure.

The gundalows rode low in the choppy water, responding sluggishly as their heavy sails caught an offshore breeze. To Caleb, the return trip seemed endless, but they reached Portsmouth harbor and moored before twilight.

Townspeople lined the dock. Women and children were there, Caleb noticed, and for the first time he realized that they had not been in evidence earlier in the day. Their cheers and huzzas revived Caleb's spirits. He saw that, all about him, men were straightening their backs and beginning to smile again as they shouted and waved back at the crowd.

Only Zeb seemed quiet and withdrawn. And so he remained. During all the work of unloading powder barrels and placing them in waiting oxcarts, Zeb did not break his silence. He did his share of work, for he did not want to attract attention, but when the last barrel was unloaded and the last oxcart had trundled away to its unknown destination, Zeb stood off by himself in the gathering dusk.

Caleb and Eli approached him. "I'm told we're to bed down for the night in Stoodley's Tavern," Caleb said. "Will ye come with us?"

Zeb regarded him suspiciously. "Is that an order?"

Caleb hesitated. "In truth," he said, "Captain McClary did ask us to keep an eye on you. I'll not deny that."

"It's an order, then. I have small choice."

"Don't think I relish your company," Eli growled. "If 'twas my say-so, I'd have ye spend the night in jail or the stocks. It makes no difference."

Zeb's smile was twisted. "But it's not your say-so." He bowed with exaggerated politeness. "I accept your kind offer. For the sake of a night's rest in Master Stoodley's feather bed, I'll bear with your bad manners."

Eli guffawed. "Feather bed! Let's hope for a vacant space on the taproom floor. Now get a move on."

"I'll move when I want," Zeb said coldly. "If I don't want to move, I'll not move."

"It's your move right now," Eli shouted, "or the tip of my boot will help ye on your way!"

After one startled look at Eli's flushed face, it was obvious to Zeb that the bandy-legged one intended to put his words into action. Zeb moved forward quickly, out of range of the promised boot tip.

Caleb struggled to hold back the laughter that suddenly bubbled in his throat. What a day this had been! He was cold, hungry, and aching in every muscle. Certainly there was little reason for laughter. Only a hysterical woman would laugh at a time like this, he told himself sternly. Yet the laughter would not be silenced. It rushed past his lips in strangled gasps as he attempted to choke it back. Beneath Zeb's suspicious scrutiny, Caleb choked and coughed and choked again. He doubled over in a paroxysm of coughing. Through tears that filled his eyes, he was surprised to see that Eli too had suddenly doubled over. The two of them coughed and coughed together.

Only Zeb seemed unaffected. "We'd best get to Stoodley's," he observed gravely, "lest you two expire of the night vapors." He watched, perplexed, as his remark seemed to redouble their paroxysms. "You planning to choke to death?" he demanded. There was a hopeful note in his voice. But it was a vain hope. Choking and gasping, Caleb and Eli found their way to Stoodley's Tavern. Zeb glowered as he followed them into the warm taproom. His day would come.

9

Caleb had a confused awakening. He had been dreaming that he was home, asleep in his own bed. Suddenly someone was shaking him by the shoulder, shouting, "Wake up! Wake up! He's flew the coop!" It must be Gramp shouting at him, Caleb thought fuzzily, as he rose to a sitting position, his eyes still half closed. What was happening? Had the old rooster flown away? No need to be so excited over that. Caleb forced his eyes wide open and for a moment looked in disbelief at his surroundings. This wasn't his bedroom. What was he doing, sitting on this hard floor?

Again the deep voice shouted in his ear. "Ye hear me? I say he's flew the coop!"

Caleb's eyes focused on the speaker. This wasn't Gramp, not this bald, ugly man. Eli, of course! The events of the preceding day came back to him in a rush.

He looked about the room—at the huddled men lying on the floor around him, barely distinguishable in the gray dawn light filtering through the tavern windows. The sleepers on both sides of him were stirring, now, and grumbling as Eli's booming boice awakened them.

"What's to be done?" Eli demanded.

"To be done about what?"

"Zeb's gone!" Eli shouted.

Caleb was fully awake now. He glanced sharply toward the nearby floor space that Zeb had occupied last evening. The space was vacant now. Caleb rubbed his eyes. "If he's gone, he's gone," he said in a husky, sleep-thickened voice. "Seems he cares naught for our company."

"Nor do I prefer his," Eli responded. "But what's he up to?" He glanced worriedly toward steps leading to the second floor of the tavern. "I'd like Captain McClary's counsel, but he's upstairs sleeping the day away."

A tousle-haired farmer lying beside Caleb propped himself up on one elbow. "So would we all," he muttered, "but for your chatter."

Eli glared at him. "By thunder, there's more to do this day than sleep."

This remark prompted widespread grumbling throughout the room, but Caleb noticed that it also served to rouse the sleeping company. In the next few minutes, most of the men were on their feet, stretching and yawning.

Caleb joined several other early risers using the washhouse facilities at the rear of the tavern. Returning to the taproom, his nose wrinkled in appreciation as the unmistakable aroma of fresh-baked bread and apple pies wafted from the bake oven at the side of the huge fireplace. As his stomach rumbled in anticipation of food, Caleb realized that he had given it precious little nourishment during the past twenty-four hours. "Quiet," he urged. "Relief is on the way."

Eli, standing beside him, gave Caleb a puzzled look.

Caleb grinned. "Pay me no heed. I'm talking to my stomach."

Eli nodded. " 'Tis the polite thing to do. For I hear your stomach talking to you."

Eli brightened as he caught sight of McClary slowly descending the stairs. "Must be the Captain's been speaking to his stomach, too," he said, as he rushed forward to meet him at the foot of the stairs. Caleb quickly followed.

"Good day, captain," Eli greeted him. "Did ye rest well?"

McClary smiled. "Well enough. And you?"

"Too well, I fear," Caleb said quickly. "Zeb left while we slept." He watched intently for McClary's reaction.

The Captain raised his eyebrows. "So? I can't say I'm surprised. Given the chance, I'd have done the same, in his place. He wasn't the most popular one amongst us."

"I fear he'll make us trouble," Eli said glumly.

"There's naught he can do now," McClary assured him. "We've set ourselves in more trouble than Zeb could dream of." He slapped Caleb on the shoulder. "Raise your chin from your bootstraps, lad. This is none of your doing. My guess is that Zeb's one desire is to shake the dust of this town from his feet. He's no doubt heading for home, fast as he can make it."

"If ye think so?" Eli said dubiously.

"I do," McClary assured him, "though thinking on an empty stomach's a chancy thing at best. Let's see what vittles the cook's prepared."

Eli winked at Caleb. "You see? Didn't I tell ye the Captain's been consulting with his stomach?"

Never did a meal taste so good to Caleb—perhaps because, as he acknowledged to himself, never had he been so hungry. There was fresh-baked bread, thickly crusted, with golden butter melted on its surface; porridge with thick cream; spicy wedges of apple pie; steaming coffee, with maple sugar for sweetening; slices of fried ham, curled and crispy at the edges. By the time they had finished, the clear December sun was shining full and bright through the small-paned tavern windows. It was going to be a good day, Caleb thought. His spirits had surged as his stomach filled.

Now, as he arose from the long bench on which he had been sitting, he noted that the room was thronged with men, all of whom seemed to share his rising sense of excitement. He moved toward Langdon and McClary, who stood next to the huge fireplace in the far corner of the big room.

"No," Langdon was saying vehemently as Caleb joined the group surrounding him, "I see no advantage in confronting the Governor. What would ye say to him?"

"I know what I'd say," a thin man in buckskins drawled in a nasal voice. "I'd say, 'Johnny, is it true that British lobsterbacks are sailing for Portsmouth?'"

"What's the sense in that?" Langdon asked reasonably. "We already have information that the British ships are about to leave Boston. We know which ships are sailing— the *Scarborough* and the *Canceaux*, with about one hundred marines aboard. They'll anchor off Great Island to protect the fort."

"They can protect what's left of it," McClary growled, "and small good it will do them."

"I say let's have the word direct from Wentworth himself," the thin man stubbornly insisted.

Langdon glared at him. "I say no. Why borrow trouble? The only purpose of such a visit would be to infuriate the Governor." He paused and cleared his throat. "Speaking for myself," he said in a lower voice, "I find many good traits in the man, though I'll not kneel to the rule he represents."

There was a murmur of assent from the crowd. Governor Wentworth still retained a measure of his popularity, although it had been badly undermined when he had sent New Hampshire carpenters to Boston to work under the direction of General Gage. Still, Caleb knew that it was hard to dislike a governor who had been born in New Hampshire; a man who, although trained to be an aristocrat, loved to dress in buckskin and walk the forest trails near his summer home in Wolfeborough.

Captain McClary nodded. "I'm agreed. We all of us here know that the true provincial government's the one we've formed in Exeter. Maybe now Wentworth will believe that too. His Council won't amount to this." He snapped his big fingers.

There was a whoop from the crowd. "When do we show 'em, Andy?" someone shouted.

"Tonight," McClary promised. "Tonight we'll show 'em. Now let us through. We've some consulting to do with our friends."

The group opened for them. Caleb watched as Langdon and McClary passed out the door and walked slowly down Market Square.

"Judging from their direction," Eli observed, "they're heading toward Tom Pickering's house at South Mill Bridge."

"What's to do now?" Caleb asked.

"Await orders," Eli retorted. "That's the main part of soldiering—just waiting around for the action to start."

Caleb and Eli stayed close to Market Square that morning, mingling with a growing throng of armed men who had traveled here from all the neighboring towns: Durham, Exeter, Lee, New Market, Epping, Stratham, Greenland, Rye. Rough mastmen from upcountry, slow-talking farmers, solid merchants in sober garb, a sprinkling of militia officers in military dress. The throng milled about the square, imbuing Caleb with a sense of rising excitement. Talk grew louder and more vehement, as the crowd partook of an apparently inexhaustible supply of rum. Most of the talk dealt with a second visit to the fort, proposed for this night, for the purpose of removing the smaller cannon and all of the muskets. It was obvious that all were eager to go. Caleb observed that there were many more men here than had been present on the previous day, and more were arriving by the minute. This promised to be a day to remember.

Toward noon, Eli, who had been fretting most of the morning as he awaited the arrival of Major Sullivan, suddenly brightened. "There he is!" he announced, pointing toward the tavern steps where Sullivan stood, talking intently to a group of men. The Major was trimly dressed in the blue uniform of a militia officer, with silver-braided hat cocked at a jaunty angle. Eli hurried, and as he was clutching Caleb's arm the boy was forced to hurry also. Eli's toothless grin widened. "By gravy, it's old home day. There's the Reverend Adams from Durham with the Major."

Reverend Adams, a lanky, solemn figure in clerical black, nodded curtly to Eli and Caleb as they approached. Eli beamed up at him, apparently not intimidated by the pastor's austere manner. "Howdy, Reverend. Come to give your blessing to the proceedings?"

"If there be need of it," the clergyman replied in a dry

voice. "Till the day comes when we can beat our swords into plowshares, I will fight the good fight."

Eli blinked. "You hear that?" he demanded of Caleb. "Ain't that the prettiest talk you ever heard?"

Reverend Adams sighed. "Thank you, Eli, but I fear the time has come for more than talk."

"The Reverend means just that," Major Sullivan told them. "He's come to share our common danger."

Eli guffawed. "Considering the present state of your pulpit, Reverend, mayhap ye think this the lesser danger. When I think of the size hole I dug beneath that pulpit—"

He paused in confusion, flushing, as both Sullivan and Adams glared at him.

Caleb watched this byplay in bewilderment. "Why a hole beneath the pulpit?" he began to question.

"Hush," Sullivan commanded fiercely. He turned to Eli. "Your blabber and blather will be the ruination of us all."

Eli was crestfallen. "I didn't think. Forget I spoke," he said to Caleb. "Dismiss it from yer mind."

"Easier said than done," Reverend Adams retorted. "So long as the lad has heard this much—with your permission, Major, ought he not to hear the rest? No telling what wild thoughts are planted in his mind."

"I suppose," Sullivan sourly agreed. He looked cautiously about him, and putting his mouth close to Caleb's ear, spoke in a barely audible voice. "The hole Eli refers to is the main reason I'm so tardy in reaching Portsmouth. There's gunpowder concealed there, beneath the pulpit of our meeting house at Durham Falls, barrels and barrels of it. 'Tis one of the main hiding places for the powder you took from the fort. 'Twas taken there by oxcart last night."

"I'll keep a closed mouth." Caleb promised.

"I'm sure you will," Reverend Adams agreed. Caleb was

surprised to see a warm smile suddenly light the parson's face and as suddenly disappear. "At least," he confided to Caleb, "thought of the gunpowder should help temper my sermons. I dare not preach hellfire and brimstone near such explosive stuff."

Caleb grinned in appreciation. Evidently the clergyman's austere manner concealed a lively humor.

The Reverend turned to Sullivan. "And, John, lest I forget, three of our men would like a word with you concerning your plans. I bid them await you on the steps of North Church." He nodded toward a large church facing the square.

Sullivan laughed. "By habit or instinct, Reverend, you do keep your flock near to the church. Lead on."

Left to themselves, Caleb and Eli wandered again among the crowd. As noontime approached, they headed for Stoodley's Tavern, where, on the steps, they saw a cluster of men surrounding the grim-faced tavern keeper. He was glaring at an official-looking document that crackled as he clutched it tightly.

"What message did Atkinson's lackey bring ye?" a bearded member of the crowd shouted.

"It's a call for volunteers," Stoodley answered disdainfully. "I suppose I must read it to ye." He cleared his throat and in a loud voice said, "This communication's addressed to Captain Dennett, here, beside me"—he nodded toward a dejected-looking young officer who wore the blue coat of the militia—"and also addressed to me, as Commission Officer of the First Regiment of Militia in the Province of New Hampshire. It reads: 'Gentlemen. You are without delay out of your several Companies to enlist or impress thirty effective men to serve his Majesty as a guard and protection to his Fort William and Mary at New Castle and make return immediately to me of your doings therein with the names of persons so enlisted, that provision may be made for their being regularly placed in the said garrison, for all of which this is your warrant. I am, Gentlemen, your friend, etc. Theodore Atkinson, Maj. Gen.'"

Stoodley looked up from the paper and searched the crowd, which had become strangely silent. "Are there any volunteers?" The crowd remained quiet, staring back at Stoodley as if offering a personal challenge. "So be it," Stoodley said gruffly. He turned to Captain Dennett. "What say you, Captain?"

The Captain's voice was high. "We should, I suppose, beat the drum for volunteers."

Suddenly a Yankee drawl broke the silence. "I'll volunteer—to tar and feather old Atkinson!"

That eased the tension. With whoops and shouts, the crowd pushed forward and clustered tightly around the two men on the steps.

"We must obey the order," Dennett said uneasily. "Is there a drummer here?"

Sullivan looked around. "Where's Tommy? Someone fetch Tommy."

In short order a lad of thirteen, with hair the color of sun-bleached hay, appeared on the run. His drum, suspended from broad shoulder straps, bounced against his stomach. "Here, sir," he panted.

Stoodley smiled at him. "Good lad." He turned to Dennett. "Now, who will make the proclamation?"

Dennett cleared his throat. "You have the louder voice, Jim."

"For this particular proclamation," Stoodley said judiciously, "I'm of the opinion that a weak voice would be far better." He winked at Tom. "And a weak drum roll, too. Let me see how soft you can beat the drum."

The boy looked puzzled. "A soft beat, sir?"

"Aye," Stoodley answered. "Just the tick of the stick on the drumhead."

Tentatively Tommy patted his drum with the stick. "Like that, sir?"

"Well done," Stoodley agreed. "What say you? For mutual support, let's both follow this drummer boy about town and make our proclamation jointly."

Captain Dennett grinned. He made his voice hoarse. "I'm that full of the quinsy, I scarce can speak."

They started out together behind the drummer, who stepped out smartly, raising his drumsticks high in the air. But Caleb noted that when they struck the drumhead they made scarcely a sound.

The trio returned within the hour and entered the tavern, where Stoodley rested his arms on a high writing desk at the side of the taproom and wrote on the back of Atkinson's order: *Pursuant to the within Warrant we have paraded the streets, caused the drums to be beat, and proclamation to be made at all the publick corners, and on the Place of Parade. No person appearing to enlist, we wait for further orders.* After he and Dennett had signed, he folded the sheet in three parts. The message was dispatched to Theodore Atkinson's palatial home, care of Tommy the drummer. "Mayhap they'll hand you a sweetmeat for your trouble," Stoodley told the boy.

Dennett smiled. "More likely you'll receive a cuff on the ear."

"I'm a nimble dodger," Tommy assured him.

Eli, sitting at a table with Caleb, caught this last remark. "So must we all be in these times," he muttered. "There's the quick and the dead."

By late afternoon, word reached the square that several gundalows were moored at dockside, below Spring Market, one of them, it was said, being Major Sullivan's boat that Eleazer Bennett had just sailed down Oyster River. Caleb and Eli, in the forefront of a crowd that surged down to the docks when the news was received, found Sullivan's boat with no difficulty. The Major was standing on the dock beside it, talking with a group in which Caleb recognized McClary and Pickering.

"And there's Eleazer," Eli said, pointing to a hulking man in greatcoat and fur cap, standing next to McClary. Eli strode up and whacked Bennett on the back. "Ye made it!" he exclaimed.

Bennett winced. "I did. And if ye don't break my back, I hope to make it home again."

Eli beamed at him. "Forgive me, friend. Ofttimes I forget the great strength of my right arm."

"One more whack such as that," Eleazer promised, "and you'll feel the great strength of my knuckles—right on the tip of your nose."

"Easy, easy," Sullivan interrupted. "I'll have need of your services for this night's work. Pray contain yourselves."

Caleb looked with admiration at the gundalow. "How many of us will this craft bear, Major?"

Sullivan regarded him quizzically for a moment and then, with sudden decision, drew Caleb aside. "You'll not be going with us tonight, Caleb," he said regretfully. "You've been put in jeopardy once, and I'll not see you endangered again. Your pa would never forgive us."

"You expect trouble?" Caleb asked in a low voice.

"Not from the garrison. Cochran's men, I hear, have been removed. But British troops are sailing up from Boston. If we meet, there'll be real trouble."

"I am that itchy to see the fort again—" Caleb began.

"Scratch that itch in Portsmouth," Sullivan interrupted sternly. "I want your word on it, lad, that you'll stay behind tonight."

Caleb could see that the Major was in dead earnest. Reluctantly he nodded. "If that's the way you'd have it."

Caleb kept his word. At ten that night, by the light of a

December moon only two days away from full, he watched the line of gundalows depart. There were four boats, each carrying a group of armed men. Caleb watched them sail slowly on the outgoing tide, down a ribbon of moonlight reflected in dark, dimpled harbor water. He watched until they were lost to sight in the star-studded night. Then he turned and walked disconsolately back to the tavern.

There were not many left behind to share the taproom floor this night—mostly the old, the ill, and lame. Caleb found no pleasure in their company. Soon he wrapped himself in his blanket and lay down in a shadowed corner of the big room. At floor level, the fumes of pipe smoke and rum were not so strong. A murmur of conversation, punctuated by frequent oaths and rare bursts of laughter, washed over him. He twisted this way and that, attempting to adjust his bony frame to hard floor boards, as events of the day tumbled through his mind. I'll not sleep a wink, he thought, staring wide-eyed at layers of tobacco smoke that swirled around the tavern ceiling.

"Not a wink—" he repeated drowsily. As his eyes slowly closed, strange figures and faces formed themselves in the tobacco haze. Eli was there, silently laughing, a wide toothless grin stretching from ear to ear. The haze shifted and there was Captain Cochran, an evil wraith with upraised sword in hand. Caleb's eyes closed altogether, and these wraithlike figures took possession of his dreams.

He awoke with a start, as loud whoops resounded in the taproom. Through sleep-dimmed eyes, Caleb saw that the room was stirring with activity, although no streak of outside light was yet visible through the windows.

"They're here! They're back!" he heard, and suddenly was on his feet with a bound. The gundalows must be back from the fort! Quickly Caleb joined the press of men jostling through the tavern door. Down the rutted street, bathed in moonlight, they hastened to the docks.

There, as the first streaks of dawn softened the night,

Caleb saw four heavily loaded gundalows at their moorings. As he pressed forward to the dock edge, he sucked in his breath. Loaded aboard each gundalow, with no attempt at concealment, were the cannon from the fort!

The next moment, Eli was at his side. An Eli cold and wet, with dark circles under his eyes, and a day's growth of stubble on his face. But his voice, as he shouted at Caleb, seemeed surprisingly vibrant. "Got 'em, by the mighty! Sixteen four-pounders! You see 'em, boy?"

Caleb nodded, speechless.

"Heavy laden we are," Eli rushed on, "but we timed it well. Sailed back from the fort on the flow and docked before the turn of the tide."

Caleb spoke with an effort. "You planned it right. Is there aught else you brought back?"

"By the bald-headed Susan, I'll say there be!" Eli exclaimed. "There's bayonets, and bags of shot, cartouche boxes, and a few dozen muskets." He made a wry face. "Though what kind of soldiers there was at the fort, I don't know. The sea air played hob with the muskets. Their only worth now is to use as clubs."

"Sounds like ye stripped the place clean."

"Not quite. There's a fine train of forty-two-pounders at the fort—the big ones. They're too heavy to carry away. But they can be dumped into the sea."

"You'll return to the fort?" Caleb asked.

Eli looked about him carefully and lowered his voice. "There's some amongst us would be pleasured, but the Major's of a different mind. Seems the British are on their way, and he daren't risk it. There's a difference of opinion, ye might say."

From the end of the dock, Caleb heard McClary's bull voice shouting, "Stand back from the boats! Guard detail! Where's my Exeter and Durham units?"

Eli pushed Caleb away from the dock edge as several men with muskets responded to McClary's call. "We'd best stand back," Eli said. "These boats will be under guard till we sail 'em upriver on the turn of the tide this afternoon."

Caleb was puzzled. "Ye'll leave the cannon in plain sight all day?"

"Why not?" Eli asked casually. "The town's in our hands. Or will be, till Gage's troops come—if they ever do. Who's to bother us?"

For the first time, the enormity of their deed struck Caleb. It was true. They had indeed taken over a town— not just any town, but the seat of New Hampshire's provincial government! They had defied the Royal Governor, sacked the King's fort. And at this point in time, there was no legal authority strong enough to say them nay. Caleb gulped. In the King's eyes, this was armed revolt. This was anarchy. What would be his answer?

10

By 8 A.M. it was obvious that it would take all of Major Sullivan's powers of persuasion to prevent the growing throng of armed men from making another assault on the fort. During the early morning hours, they had been streaming into town, converging on the square—at least a thousand of them—all primed for action. From his experience of the past two days, Caleb realized how easily these men could be transformed into an unruly mob. They milled about, left to their own devices, as the leaders of the previous night's raid obtained needed rest.

To Caleb's relief, Sullivan, McClary, Langdon, and Pickering appeared on the tavern steps within the hour.

They were met with loud cheers as more and more of the men in the street became aware of their presence. Caleb took note of the leaders' drawn expressions.

Eli squinted anxiously at Sullivan. "My Major looks frazzled."

Caleb nodded. "So do they all." They must have been consulting together, he thought. Perhaps some announcement would be made. But the leaders remained silent as they slowly descended the steps and separated, each mingling with a different part of the crowd.

Caleb and Eli rushed to join the men surrounding Sullivan. "I ask you to return to your homes," they heard him say in a weary voice. Slowly he enumerated his reasons. This must be the way he is as a lawyer, arguing a case in court, Caleb thought. Unemotionally, logically, Sullivan laid fact on fact. The crowd was quieting now, paying close attention. The British ships were coming, Sullivan pointed out. A direct meeting with the redcoats might lead to bloodshed. And there was no need for it. The task set by the Committee of Safety had been accomplished. The fort's powder and arms had been taken. Now he entreated his good friends to return peaceably to their homes.

The men grumbled and shouted questions. The Major answered patiently, with good humor, calling some questioners by name and jesting with them. Caleb could feel the tension lessen.

"He's a born persuader," Caleb whispered to Eli.

"Aye," Eli glumly agreed. "Ding blast him. I'd like one more trip to that fort." It was evident from Eli's tone that he felt such a trip was becoming a remote possibility.

The other leaders must have been equally persuasive, for by midmorning the crowd began to disperse. Many reasons were given—unfinished chores, worried families, a long road home—but no one voiced the thought that must have been present in every mind. The warning that they might meet a trained force of British soldiers had undoubtedly been a sobering one.

How would I fare, Caleb thought, facing a rank of the King's Own with fixed bayonets? He had conducted himself well at the fort, he knew, but overcoming a token defense made by a handful of frightened men could not be called a true test. He realized well enough the low opinion that British officers held of the colonial militia. If it came to a showdown, the British said, one charge of grapeshot would scatter the country bumpkins. Caleb doubted this, but a gnawing worry remained in his mind. He had heard lead whistling overhead when assaulting the fort, but, unlike the veterans among them, he and the other young men had never really been tested under sustained fire. Perhaps this doubt was nagging them, too. No matter. The question would not be resolved this day. Their leaders had dissuaded them from a direct test of arms. Secretly, Caleb was glad.

Toward noon Captain McClary found Caleb and Eli warming themselves before the tavern's great fireplace. "There you are," he said. "You're harder to find than fleas on a sheep dog." He seated himself with a sigh on the settle before the hearth and extended his hands toward the warmth radiating from great crackling logs. "I'm used up, and that's a fact. Labor all night; argue half the day. And now I've a long ride home to Epsom."

Eli frowned. "There's something amiss at home?"

"I hope not," McClary answered. "But I'm that anxious to see my wife and sprats, I can't abide more delay. My task here is done. With your help, Eli, the Major will see that the cannon are brought upriver on the incoming tide. The town's quiet. We've convinced our friends to return home. And now I've convinced myself of the same." He turned to Caleb. "I'd consider it a favor if you'd accompany me. You could ride back on the horse I loaned you, and lead my horse that Zeb rode to town."

"Of course, if I can help," Caleb agreed. "But if there's no more need of me here—"

"Go, lad," Eli urged. "You've done your share, and more. I'll miss ye, for your company pleasures me. But we'll meet again."

Caleb managed a grin. "When there's another fort to assault?"

Eli winked. "Mayhap. These are parlous times."

"Good-by, Eli," McClary said gravely, "and I'll see that you receive the wig I promised."

Eli felt his bald head. "What with all the fuss and hub-bub, I've been forgetful of my old egg head. I'll be thankful for that wig." In sudden remembrance he added, "And don't forget the new hat ye promised."

"You sound like an Indian," McClary said gravely. "You want to keep your wigwam."

Eli puzzled over this remark. "My wigwam?" Suddenly he guffawed. "My wig warm! By hokey, Captain, you're the clever one. Ye get that, Caleb? I want to keep my wigwam!"

"I don't think I do," Caleb said innocently. "Perhaps if 'twas explained to me—"

McClary leaped to his feet. "Come on," he said roughly, grasping Caleb's arm and leading him off, just in time to forestall a long exposition.

"I'll explain it out to ye when I see ye again," Eli shouted after them.

The rutted, snow-crusted road leading to Captain Mc-Clary's home in Epsom seemed a familiar one to Caleb. Having traveled it once, in the opposite direction, he found it easy riding, even though he was leading the horse that Zeb had ridden.

They reached the McClary farm at nightfall. The Captain received a tumultuous greeting from six of his children, who rushed to him the moment he stepped inside the door and clung like limpets to his coat, breeches, and legs. The youngest, two year old Nancy, bounced in her mother's arms, straining toward her father. Dragging his clinging brood with him, McClary reached his wife in three great strides, encompassing her and Nancy in a bear hug.

Caleb, standing unnoticed for the moment, felt his throat tighten. Suddenly he too yearned to be home, surrounded by loved ones.

A moment later, the Captain noticed Caleb standing dejectedly alone. "Unhand me, ye sprats," he ordered, "and give a proper welcome to my friend, Caleb Stark."

Caleb forced a grin to match that of the oldest boy, Jim, who dutifully shook his hand and welcomed him. Andrew and John followed suit. The three youngest continued clinging tightly to their father's breeches and stared wide-eyed at their guest.

The Captain squeezed his wife's waist. "It's good to be home, Mrs. McClary. Ye don't know how I've looked forward to this moment—a warm welcome, a warm supper, a warm toddy, and my own warm bed."

His wife laughed. "Sounds as if you're chilled clean through. Sit down, now, you and Caleb. Your warm supper's waiting to be spooned out."

"Did ever a man have such a wife?" McClary demanded of Caleb. "She anticipates my every wish." He sighed. "With such a home as this, it does seem a pity to leave so soon again."

Quickly Mrs. McClary stepped away from her husband and deposited Nancy on the floor. Her hands rested on her hips. "And what does that mean?"

The Captain smiled uneasily. "Why, simply that I must accompany our young friend home tomorrow. He travels a hard path to Dunbarton." His voice trailed away as he met his wife's level gaze.

"Dunbarton, is it?" she said in a tight voice. "Do you

know how long I've been alone with this brood, worrying myself half to death, while you go traipsing off, fighting and carrying on and engaging in mischief I can only guess at?"

"Easy, my love," McClary urged. " 'Twill only be a day's journey."

"I can make it alone," Caleb said quickly. "Pray don't trouble yourself."

The Captain's lips tightened. "It's no trouble, lad. I'd not forgive myself, were you to meet with a mishap for lack of company."

"Lack of company!" his wife explained. "I'm the one lacking company." She would have pursued the matter, but a close look at the firm set of her husband's jaw dissuaded her. With a sigh, she turned toward the fireplace. "I'll not argue more. It's food ye need now, not shrewish talk. It's just that I worry so. And we do have such need of ye—"

McClary placed his hands on his wife's shoulder and swung her about. She faced him squarely, her eyes brimming with tears. "Laws o' mercy," McClary said softly, "ye know I'd dearly desire to spend all my days here at my home hearth. But it must be as a free man. Until that time comes—"

Mrs. McClary placed a gentle finger on her husband's lips. "I know. Dame Freedom's your second love. I must learn to accommodate her." She managed a smile. "You must forgive my wifely jealousy."

The next morning dawned bright and clear, a crisp December day. Snow-covered fields surrounding the house dazzled Caleb with their reflected brilliance as he stepped out the door, after bidding farewell to Mrs. McClary and all the children. In the distance, evergreen boughs drooped beneath their burden of sparkling snow. A pine tree at the edge of the farmyard cast its dark shadow on the snow, shadow and tree swaying in a light breeze, each pine needle etched in sunlight. The cold air had an astringent bite. It tickled Caleb's nostrils, carried an indefinable flavor of ozone to his taste buds, sent the blood racing faster through his veins.

In that moment, Caleb was a part of this day, reveling in its clarity, its pristine freshness. Savoring the frigid air and expelling it in a cloud of vapor, he could feel its tonic effect coursing through him, reaching to his extremities, tingling fingers and toes. He pushed back his shoulders and stretched upward. He would like to extend his arms outward, encompassing this rare morning.

Captain McClary, busily adjusting his snowshoes, looked up with some concern. "You have a stiff back?"

Caleb shook his head. Quickly he knelt to adjust his own snowshoes. "Just stretching," he said.

McClary watched critically as Caleb laced the rawhide thongs about his high winter moccasins. "Get 'em good and tight," he counseled. "It's going to be a long cold trip."

Caleb realized this well enough. He felt warm now, dressed like his companion in close-fitting woolen waistcoat, fringed leather jacket, leather breeches, and fur cap pulled down tight to his ears. But no matter how comfortable he might feel at this moment, fresh from the warmth of the McClary farmhouse, Caleb knew before his journey was done the cold would become a threatening force, chilling his body, sapping his vitality. He could understand the Captain's concern with details before setting out on an overland winter's journey. Careful planning was the key to survival.

Caleb rose from a kneeling position and picked up his musket. He felt McClary looking at him carefully, as though checking his equipment. Mentally, Caleb did the same. The light pack strapped to his back contained dried beef and parched corn. His powder horn was half full. A leather bag at his waist contained musket balls. He carried extra flints. A hunting knife protruded from his belt. "I'm ready," he said.

McClary nodded soberly. "I do believe you are."

Caleb grinned. This journey didn't frighten him—not with a man like McClary at his side.

The best part of going away is coming home again, Caleb decided, as he relaxed that evening in his own home, surrounded by his family. He saw his familiar surroundings with fresh eyes. The very solidity of the big house was a source of satisfaction. It was more than a tangible protection against the elements. This house gave an impression of permanence and integrity and pride in craftsmanship that reflected the character of its owner.

Looking across the room at the seamed, weathered face of his grandfather, Caleb smiled at him. "It's good to be back," he said softly.

John Stark, seated opposite his son, raised a questioning eyebrow. "So? You've had your fill of adventuring?"

Caleb nodded. For the moment, he'd had his fill and then some. It had been a long, cold trek he and Captain McClary had made that day to Dunbarton. Although, thanks to the Captain's knowledge of the trails, the journey had been uneventful, it had seemed endless to Caleb. How he had yearned to be home! There was so much to tell. So many adventures to share. To share. Aye, that was the important thing.

It had been a wonderful surprise to find his father, mother, and brother Archie at Gramp's house, waiting for him, unwilling to return to their own home in Derryfield until they were sure of his safe return. There had been some worrisome moments, his father told him, especially after young Zeb had returned home on the previous day. Zeb had spread wild tales of insurrection and had intimated that Caleb and his companions were hunted men.

Now, sitting around the massive fireplace, warmed by

a crackling blaze, John Stark wished to know the true state of affairs. He put the question directly to his old friend, McClary. "Is there a price on your head?" he demanded.

McClary puffed deliberately on his clay pipe for a moment before answering. Caleb could feel tension growing in the room. Gram's specially constructed chair creaked as, readjusting her great bulk, she leaned forward. His mother and young brother Archie also were looking expectantly toward the Captain.

At length McClary gravely nodded. "That could well be true."

John Stark's ice-blue eyes drilled into those of his friend. "And is there a price on my son's head?"

McClary returned his gaze unflinchingly. "That also could be true. For Caleb helped storm the fort." A grim smile flickered over his face as he added, "If so, he's in good company. I hear the Governor has summoned his Council and stripped Langdon and Sullivan of their commissions in the militia. I have no doubt I'll also be included in that order, along with all the other officers who helped us. Plus any government officials he can identify. He's already deprived two of our men of their commissions as Justices of the Peace."

John Stark's face showed deep concern as he turned to Caleb. "I blame myself," he said hoarsely. "I sent you on this mission. I urged your involvement."

"I involved myself," Caleb answered quickly. "No one urged me to storm the fort. Indeed," he added, glancing toward McClary, "I took good care that none of your friends saw me board the gundalow—for I knew full well I'd have been sent skeedaddling back to the tavern."

McClary nodded. "That's the truth. But once at the fort, I know one man who was glad to see ye—no matter how ye arrived." He turned to John Stark. "Your boy perhaps saved Tom Pickering's life." He told the story of Caleb's skirmish with Captain Cochran in detail, adding a few embellishments that made Caleb squirm in embarrassment. As the story concluded, Caleb saw that his father was looking at him with new respect.

"You're a Stark," his father said simply. "There's no holding back when there's action at hand. No more than I'd been held back at your age."

Molly Stark sniffed. "At his age? I can't keep you from trouble even now." She looked anxiously at Caleb. "You weren't hurt in the scuffle?"

"Nary a scratch," Caleb assured her.

"The lad's tough as bull beef," McClary quickly added.

Archie's eyes were shining. "I dearly wish I'd been there," he said in a breathless voice. His hand swept the air in simulation of a sword stroke. "Take that, Cochran. And that!"

"Archie!" his mother said reprovingly. "We don't make games of violence."

Grandfather Page snorted. "Oh, let him be, Molly. All boys are bloodthirsty. Ye talk more like a lady of the gentry than the frontier girl I reared." He turned to Caleb. "Would ye believe it, Caleb, when we first came to Dunbarton in seventeen fifty-one, yer ma stood lookout for Indians while we tilled the land? And she fetched home jugs of water from One Stack Brook with a musket in one hand and the jug in 'tother—watching the woods about her every step of the way, lest the savages snatch her scalp."

"I don't recall it was all that grim," Molly Stark protested, "but I'll grant there was no need to go search for danger. It was all about us. And I had my fill of it."

Her father snorted. "Woman talk! There's no way to advance without taking a bit of risk." He looked quickly about him. "Do ye suppose," he asked in a husky whisper, "I'd now have my hoard of golden guineas had I been content to stay within the civilized confines of Massachusetts?"

Caleb leaned eagerly forward. Only once, during all the

years he had lived in this house, had Gramp shown him his treasure. Caleb had been a small boy at the time, but he remembered every detail of the incident. Gramp, after unlocking his bedroom door with a massive key, had beckoned Caleb to kneel down beside him at the side of the bed—just as if they were about to say their prayers, Caleb had thought. Then, lifting the edge of the heavy quilt, Gramp had reached under the bed and pulled out a plain wooden half-bushel measure, heaped with golden guineas that glowed in the soft daylight filtering into the room. Caleb had been invited to run his fingers through the coins, and he could still feel their cool, smooth surfaces spilling through his hands. He did not know what obscure motive had caused his grandfather to show off his gold on that occasion. Never again had Caleb been invited behind the locked door.

Now, as Caleb listened to Gramp, he felt a growing excitement. Gramp's going to tell us how he gathered together his golden guineas, he thought. Perhaps he had battled a buccaneer for pirate gold. Perhaps—

Caleb's romantic imaginings were stopped in mid-flight by Gram's deep voice. "Your store of golden guineas, Mr. Page," she said severely, "was started because you have a preference for well-fleshed wives." Unexpectedly she began to laugh. She wobbled and bobbled and shook her chair. Beneath his feet, Caleb could feel the sturdy floor boards vibrate. He looked with wonder at this leviathan of a woman whose mirth could shake a house.

Gramp also began to laugh. "You're right, Mrs. Page. By chowder, you're right. Caleb, your Grandmother refers to my first wife, may her soul rest in peace. Before we left Massachusetts, I sold my land there for my wife's weight in silver dollars. I gathered five thousand of them before the scales tipped."

Gram Page nodded. "Then he turned them all in for golden guineas. That's how the collection began."

Captain Page turned a calculating gaze on his wife. "Now, if I could strike such a trade for *this* property," he said with mock gravity, "what a price I could obtain!"

His wife took the remark in good spirit. "Always providing you could find a scale to support such a weight. Though you no doubt know the exact whereabouts of such a device." She sighed and wheezed. "You're a greedy man, Mr. Page. Sometimes I wonder how I put up with ye."

"Because you love me, my dear, just as I love every inch of your fair expanse."

Once again the floor shook as Gram Page quivered with laughter. "Which one of my lovely chins do ye love the best?" she demanded.

"All three of them," her husband promptly replied. "I can't find it in my heart to honor one above the other."

John Stark coughed dryly. "If you two lovebirds are done with your cooing, may I hark back to my original query?"

"Say on," Captain Page agreed. "What query was that, John?"

"Concerning Caleb," Stark answered patiently. "Before I leave this house, I must assure myself he's in no danger of arrest by the Sheriff's men."

Captain Page was instantly serious. "Set yer mind to rest on that score. They'll not touch the lad in this town. I'll see to that."

"I think I can assure ye, John, that the King-lovers in this province may growl, but they'll not bite," McClary added. "Not if they know what's good for them. At this point, they don't have the strength."

John Stark nodded gravely. This was assurance enough. "On the morrow, then, we travel home," he said, for he knew that Molly was yearning to be reunited with their two young daughters, who had remained behind at Derryfield in the care of a maidservant.

II

Caleb often thought in the days that followed of the faith that his father put in the words of his friends. It buoyed Caleb's own faith, for he could not quite put out of his mind the thought that one day he might be snatched away by constables.

Then, early on the last day of December, his grandfather sought him out in the barn. Caleb looked curiously at the large sheet of newsprint that Captain Page thrust toward him. "Read it," the Captain ordered. "By jinks, but Wentworth's hopping mad. These proclamations, they say, are sent out all through the province."

Slowly Caleb read the proclamation. Its official language described the assault on Fort William and Mary in a manner that made him wince. This raid, he read, had been conducted "in open Hostility and direct Oppugnation of his Majesty's Government, and in the most atrocious Contempt of his Crown and Dignity."

As for the men who had taken part in the raid, Caleb's eyes opened wide as he read:

"I Do, by Advice and Consent of his Majesty's Council, issue this Proclamation, ordering and Requiring in his Majesty's Name, all Magistrates and other officers, whether Civil or Military . . . to exert themselves in detecting and securing in some of his Majesty's Gaols in this Province the said Offenders, in Order to their being brought to condign punishment. . . . I do in the most earnest and solemn manner, exhort and enjoin you . . . to beware of suffering yourselves to be seduced by the false Art or Menaces of abandoned Men, to abet, protect, or screen from Justice any of the said high-handed Offenders, or to withhold or secrete his Majesty's Munition forcibly taken from his Castle. . . . This Injunction it is my bounden duty to lay strictly upon you . . . as you value individually your Faith and Allegiance to his Majesty . . . and as you would avert the most dreadful but most certain Consequences of a contrary conduct to yourself and Posterity.

"Given at the Council Chamber in Portsmouth, the 26th Day of December, in the 15th Year of the Reign of our Sovereign Lord George the Third, by the Grace of God, of Great Britain, and Ireland, King and Defender of the Faith, in the year of our Lord Christ, 1774.

J' Wentworth"

Caleb whistled. "What's he mean by 'condign punishment'?"

"Dunno," his grandfather replied, "but whatever it is, we want no part of it." He smiled reassuringly, so that the crinkly squint lines at his eyes almost met those extending upward from each side of his mouth, like two deep parenthesis marks. "Don't you worry, lad," he said. "Despite the fact that two shiploads of Gage's troops are finally anchored off Fort William and Mary, Wentworth still can't claim the upper hand. That's what makes him so edgy. Of course, items like this don't help much." From a pocket of his greatcoat, Captain Page withdrew a thin newspaper. "Latest issue of the Portsmouth paper, *New Hampshire Gazette and Historical Chronicle*," he announced. "Issue of Friday, December sixteenth—the day after the raid. It reads, 'We hear the People in this Province, thinking the powder at New Castle not safe, have removed it to a place of more security.'" He solemnly returned the paper to his pocket.

"That's all?" Caleb asked.

"Every smidgin. Such a small item to tell such a large tale. It's just another pinprick to anger the British. The question is, how far can they be pushed?"

"You think there may be real trouble?"

"I can't deceive ye," the old man answered. "I *know* there will be. Do ye think when the King receives word of this assault on his fort that he'll regard it lightly? My guess is, this action will anger him as naught else has. He'll demand quick action in the future from Gage's troops. There'll be no more half measures."

"Captain McClary says we'll welcome a showdown with the lobsterbacks," Caleb told him.

"So he does," his grandfather agreed. "Captain McClary still carries a youthful brashness, though past the age of youth. As for me, I'm an old man. I heed the signs and portents." He lowered his voice to a hoarse whisper. "There are those who tell of thunder in the sky, like a cannonade —and this on a clear day, with no storm near. And of shrouded shapes seen in the clouds: a bony hand holding aloft a broken sword; a grinning skull staring down. And Ahasset Nott tells of being pursued through his cornfield by a great bird with knives for talons, and a human voice, which croaked to him, "Ahasset Nott, the day is near. Repent. Repent."

Caleb barely repressed a smile as he thought of lanky Ahasset, whose fondness for hard cider was well known, running a weaving course through his cornfield. Yet he knew that he must not let Gramp suspect that he took small stock in ghostly matters. "It does appear there's a lively year ahead," Caleb said diplomatically.

"If 'lively' is the word for it," Captain Page replied. "Believe me, lad, I see no cause to celebrate the coming of 'seventy-five this midnight." He glanced sharply toward the barn door as it swung open briefly, admitting a blast of cold air.

Caleb too looked toward the open door. His eyes widened as he recognized the broad-shouldered, barrel-shaped man in bearskin coat who was now swinging the door closed behind him. Zeb's father had come to pay them a visit!

Gramp spoke through tight lips. "Morning, Mr. Snavely."

The big man grunted. He walked toward Caleb and his grandfather, regarding them warily through small, close-set eyes—eyes that Zeb had inherited, Caleb thought.

"Cold out," Thaddeus Snavely offered, standing directly before them, bulking large in his hairy black coat—an observation innocent enough but, coming from Snavely, having the tone of a challenge.

Gramp nodded agreement, looking up into the big man's face. "It may come up storming by night."

Snavely shifted his full attention to Caleb. "How do you fare, lad?" he asked gruffly.

Caleb gulped. "Well. Very well. And you?"

Snavely's mouth drew downward; his eyebrows arched upward. Never had Caleb seen such a lugubrious expression. "Poorly," he said, touching a hamlike hand to his chest. "I'm sick here."

"Dyspepsia," Gramp promptly diagnosed. "I have the same trouble."

Snavely looked annoyed. "I'm sick at heart," he said shortly. "Sick 'cause of the way my boy's been treated by your grandson." He glared accusingly at Caleb.

"Because of what I've done to Zeb?" Caleb asked unbelievingly.

Gramp scowled at the big man. "You mean, because of what your boy did to my grandson. That's enough to give anyone the dyspepsia."

"Don't you twist my words around!" Snavely shouted at him. With an effort, he regained control of his voice. "Ye both know well enough how ye seduced my lad into trouble at Portsmouth; how he was left to fend for himself on the road from Durham; how he was forced to make the return trip home, defenseless and alone."

Caleb opened his mouth to frame a denial but was stopped by Snavely's forefinger waved beneath his nose. "Do ye deny it?" he demanded.

"Lies," Gramp sputtered. "Never have I heard such a passel of lies."

Snavely turned toward him ominously. "Ye call me a liar, friend Page?" He clenched his great fist, and for a moment Caleb thought he would strike the old man. But then the fist slowly unclenched. "Ye can't anger me," Sanvely said in a thick voice. "I take that insult from whence it comes." He looked at Caleb. "I come here not to cause trouble but to begin the new year aright. We must all live together as near neighbors. So why not let bygones be bygones?" The corners of his mouth lifted in what he presumed to be a smile. "I forgive ye," he said grandly.

"You forgive *us!*" Captain Page sputtered. "By the great, ring-tailed, three-toed horn toad, you have the everlasting gall—"

"Enough!" Snavely shouted at him. "Lest I forget my good intentions." He turned to Caleb. "Zeb forgives ye, too," he said smugly. With that, he turned on his heel and quickly left the barn.

Caleb and Gramp, both red-faced and filled with violent thoughts, were momentarily speechless. They looked at each other for a long moment. Then suddenly Gramp whacked his hand upon his knee and began to laugh. He choked and laughed and choked again. "Zeb forgives us," he finally gasped.

At that, Caleb too began to laugh. In the echoing reaches of the big barn, their laughter rose, wave on wave, while the brindle cow in her stall twitched her ears and flicked her tail as she regarded these two unpredictable human creatures.

Cold mud squished through Caleb's toes as he dug parsnips in early April, walking barefoot through the oozy plot of ground that last summer had contained John Stark's vegetable garden. It was a cold, dirty task that he had assigned himself. His work breeches and jacket, though rolled tight above knees and elbows, were spattered; the exposed portions of his legs and arms were caked with mud. His hands were numb from reaching into the muck and prying loose the tapering, mud-covered parsnips. The bag he carried on his back was becoming heavy; his shoulders ached from the unaccustomed weight. And yet, Caleb was happy, for he was looking forward to the year's first meal of parsnips, sweetened by a winter spent in the frozen ground.

A New England winter is a chancy thing. It extends through March and into April. Even now, as Caleb dug in the quagmire that once had been a garden, there was a spit of snow in the air. But with his bag of fresh-picked parsnips heavy on his back, he felt that spring could not be far off.

Though chilled and dirty, he hummed a snatch of tune as he worked. He was glad to see this winter end. It had been a vexing one, filled with alarms and uncertainties—with always the thought in the back of his mind that perhaps the law would come for him. But day had followed day, and no constables had appeared. Gradually Caleb had come to accept Gramp's assurance that Wentworth might bluster but did not have the support to trade words for action.

In late March, when his pa had sent word from Derryfield that he could use help on the farm, Gramp had urged Caleb to go. "The change will do ye good," Gramp had assured him, sensing that Caleb was eager for a change, after enduring a succession of winter chores mixed with studies assigned by Reverend Pickels.

After arriving at Derryfield, Caleb had found that his tasks were just as numerous, but sharing them with his younger brother Archie seemed to break the monotony. Together they performed the seemingly unending chore of bringing in wood for the fires. Both boys helped their father fell a white pine, to be used for clapboards. They assisted a ewe that lambed in the night. Caleb brought in the last run of sap from the big maple trees in the sugar bush and helped boil it down in the sweet-smelling sugar house. The boys accompanied their father to town with a wagonload of boards he had cut at his sawmill for Will Petrie. In town, they delivered the boards, sold a quart of clover seed for twelve shillings silver, and traded off an ounce of onion seed and a gill of linseed oil. They returned home with coins jingling in the money sack, a pound of coffee, two cakes of chocolate, and a package of ginger.

Caleb was surprised to see how upset his mother became when she learned of their purchases. "Imports!" she said accusingly. "How do you expect me to stick by my resolve when you bring home such stuff?"

John Stark looked ill at ease. "I thought it would be a treat. It was available—"

"So is bohea tea," his wife reminded him. "And I've denied myself, though heaven knows I'd dearly love a cup." She tapped her foot. "And spring lamb," she added, as another thought came to her. "There's succulent, tender spring lamb available, right on this farm—and that too I've denied us, for we must raise our own wool."

Her husband nodded glumly. "You're right, Mrs. Stark. My purchases were a springtime impulse. I'll discard them. I'll throw them to the pigs." He scooped the packages off the table.

Molly Stark gasped. "You'll do no such thing! We'll not waste what is already bought."

His father winked at Caleb as he returned the items to the table. "If that's your wish, my dear."

Caleb was puzzled. "What's the harm in buying such?"

"The Continental Congress says that from now on the colonies must be self-sufficient," his father explained. "Buying imports enriches the King's treasury."

Young Archie eyed the chocolate greedily. "Let's eat the chocolate," he suggested. "Then it won't be here to tempt us."

His father tousled Archie's hair. "With a mind such as yours," he said gravely, "your vocation should be the law."

They laughed then. But thinking back on the incident now, as he carried his bag of parsnips to the well, Caleb reflected that this really was no laughing matter. The colonists had taken a stand. "We'll live by our own efforts and support ourselves without your help," they had in effect told King George. This was a brave act, Caleb thought, as he dumped his parsnips next to the well sweep. It was the act of an independent child come of age, striking out on his own. He too would come of age on his sixteenth birthday in December. Would he react in such a way? Not likely. There was no need of it in his family, for its members made an effort to understand each other. Caleb pondered this as he scrubbed the parsnips in a wooden trough by the side of the well. Perhaps if the colonies and the King would make the same effort—Caleb sighed. It was too much for him. Wiser heads than his were in command.

He carried his muddy sack to the shed entrance and propped it against the wall. He was preparing to enter the summer kitchen when fast-approaching hoofbeats drew his attention to the road. Caleb paused at the kitchen door as a high-stepping sorrel mare turned into the farmyard. Its slim, straight-backed rider headed his mount directly toward Caleb.

The lathered horse was spattered with mud from fetlock to muzzle. Its rider, also daubed with mud, reined in at the hitching rail and swung down stiffly from the saddle. Caleb, observing him curiously as he tethered his mare, guessed that he had traveled a long road. There was something peculiar about this man, Caleb decided. His garb was that of a rustic workman—gray greatcoat, leather breeches, hand-knit stockings, a handkerchief loosely knotted about his neck. But the man's walk, as he approached Caleb, was not the easy, ambling gait of a farmer. Here was a military stride—brisk and purposeful. Caleb could almost count the cadence as the stranger approached with shoulders back and head erect.

He spoke with a clipped British accent. "Is Captain Stark about?"

Caleb nodded.

"I wish to talk with him. And I'd appreciate someone looking after my mount. I fear she's quite spent."

Caleb thought that the visitor looked quite spent himself but refrained from saying so. "I'll tell the Captain," he promised, "and fetch someone to see after your horse." He indicated a rough bench outside the door. "Rest yourself."

A smile passed over the visitor's mud-daubed face. "Thank you. But it feels good to stand awhile."

Caleb found his father in the barn, where he was assisting his hired man, Tom Pickett, to replace broken teeth in a wooden hay rake. After listening carefully to Caleb's description of their strange visitor, John Stark sent Tom to take care of the man's horse and to direct their visitor to the barn.

"I don't like the sound of this," the Captain said, as Tom departed. "He sounds like a British agent. But what does he want of me?"

"Will ye talk with him?" Caleb asked.

"I'll talk to him, right enough. But not alone." With sudden decision, John Stark indicated a musket propped against a stanchion. "Take my gun. It's loaded, so be careful. And climb into the hayloft. I'll feel better, knowing you're there."

Caleb's eyes sparkled. "I'll see that nothing goes amiss."

"Good lad. I'll rely on you to keep eyes and ears open."
He frowned as Caleb hurriedly snatched the musket. "Pray
be careful. I don't need a hole blown through the shakes.
Nor through me, for that matter."

Caleb cradled the musket in his arms. "I'll treat it gentle
as a newborn babe."

John Stark's thin lips curved into a smile. "Good. I'll
attempt to treat our visitor with the same caution."

Caleb climbed the ladder and settled himself in the hayloft where he could look down through a wide crack in the
boards and obtain a reasonably clear view of his father
below. John Stark continued mending the hay rake, putting
it aside only when his visitor appeared, blinking, in the
bright rectangle of sunlight at the open barn door.

"Over here," Stark called, as he arose from the upended
keg on which he had been sitting.

The visitor cautiously entered, squinting to adjust his
eyes to the barn's shadowy interior. "Captain Stark?" he
inquired, pausing a step away. He peered suspiciously at
the lean, gaunt man in farm dress, evidently unable to rec-
oncile this simple farmer with the famed Indian fighter
he had come to meet.

"The very same," Stark assured him. "At your service,
sir."

The visitor, reassured by the brisk, decisive voice, visibly
relaxed. He glanced about him. "May I speak freely?"

"Please do." Stark indicated a keg opposite the one on
which he had been sitting. "Have a seat—such as it is."

As his visitor gingerly seated himself, Stark sat down
again and regarded him curiously.

"If ye don't mind my saying so, you've created some
interest here. Your mode of dress doesn't fit your manner
of speech."

The man flushed. "Easy to see I'm not cut out for the
role of master spy." He smiled briefly. "It's not much of a

disguise, is it? But, I dare say, better than a British uniform in these parts." He extended his hand. "I'm Captain Gilchrist of the Fourth Regiment."

"The King's Own," John Stark remarked as he shook hands. "A fine regiment."

The British officer regarded him seriously. "Your old commanding officer in the Rangers, Colonel Rogers, thinks so. I bear a message from him to you."

Stark frowned. "Bob Rogers? The last I heard, he was having all sorts of trouble in England and was sent to debtor's prison."

"A set of unfortunate misunderstandings," Gilchrist said uncomfortably. "Least said, soonest mended. At present, due to the intercession of Lord Dartmouth, your old friend has been granted a pardon. He's been given full retirement pay of a major and is making ready to sail back to America."

Stark raised his eyebrows. "So? Sounds as if, now that you need him here, you're willing to let bygones be bygones."

"I have been instructed to hand you this message from him, sir," Gilchrist said stiffly. From an inner pocket of his greatcoat, he withdrew a crackling sheet of paper and gave it to Stark.

Holding it toward a moted shaft of sunlight that filtered through a small, cobwebbed window, Stark read the document. "It's Rogers' hand, right enough," he announced at length. "And I suppose I'd have to admit the sentiments expressed are his own, too." Slowly he lowered the paper. "Rogers never was much for politics," he said in a surprisingly soft voice. "He craves action, and the cause which gives him an excuse is of minor importance. The trouble is, he's a few years behind the times."

"I understand him to be an astute man," the British officer said diplomatically, "though I've never had the pleasure of meeting him."

"You'll have that pleasure soon enough," Stark assured him, "if he comes back this summer—as he promises in this letter—and forms a Ranger company loyal to the King." He grimaced. "Poor Rogers. I hate to see him come home." Slowly he raised his ice-blue eyes to meet the gaze of Captain Gilchrist. "As for me assisting in the formation of such a company, you must realize that's out of the question."

Gilchrist's eyes wavered beneath the steady gaze. "A pity." With an effort, he met Stark's gaze directly again. He spoke slowly. "General Gage thinks highly of you. If you were to assist us in our efforts, the General is prepared to offer you the rank of full colonel."

John Stark's lips formed a noiseless whistle. "I didn't think to be valued so highly! Convey my thanks to your General—and also, of course, my refusal."

Captain Gilchrist stood up. He bowed stiffly and extended his hand for the message from Rogers. "If I may have that back, sir."

Stark handed the message to him. "As you will. It means naught to me. My old comrade speaks a strange language these days."

"A true language, sir. Perhaps you would do well to heed it."

To Caleb's surprise, his father did not appear angered by this remark. Instead, his expression was sad as he said in a low voice, "Perhaps we should all make a greater effort at understanding. Though I fear it's too late in the day for such action."

Gilchrist's voice was impatient. "I take it, sir, that your refusal is final?"

Stark frowned at the tone of voice. "Yes, by Harry," he snapped. "You have my final refusal. And tell your General to send no more recruiters to my door."

The young officer involuntarily backed off a pace. "As you wish, sir." He left hurriedly, not wishing to put the patience of this unpredictable man to a further test.

John Stark glared after him, "Arrogance!" he growled, watching the officer stride across the farmyard, snatch the reins of his horse from the hired man, and gallop off.

Caleb climbed down from the hayloft and replaced the musket against a stanchion. John Stark's anger faded as he looked at Caleb. "How would ye like a British colonel for a pa?" he asked.

Caleb managed a grin. "If it's all the same to you, I prefer ye as you are."

Stark nodded. "My opinion exactly. I get into enough trouble, without looking for it."

"It seems trouble comes looking for you." Caleb remarked.

His father considered this. "It does at that. Perhaps, in these times, trouble comes to all of us who don't hide our heads in the sand." He glanced up as the hired man looked into the barn.

" 'Pears as though the young gent left in an awful yank," Tom Pickett observed.

"It does indeed," Stark agreed. He looked about him. "Come in, Tom. I do believe we deserve a drink of cider after all this to-do. If I can find the jug."

Quickly Tom fetched the jug from a shadowed corner of the barn. "It jest so happens I remember where it's at."

"So I see," Stark said gravely. "Help yourself, Tom."

The hired man lifted the neck of the earthen jug to his lips and took a great gulp.

"Have another swallow," Stark urged, as Tom wiped his mouth with the back of his hand.

"Don't mind if I do," Tom agreed. "Like my pa used to say, 'One drink is like sittin' on a one-legged stool.' " He took another long swallow and passed the jug to his employer.

Caleb took the next swig. This was a celebration, of a sort. Caleb wasn't sure just what it was they were celebrating: Pa's refusal of a British commission, perhaps. But mostly, Caleb felt, they were toasting an uncertain future.

12

The complexion of that uncertain future was abruptly changed on the afternoon of April 19, as news reached Derryfield of events that had taken place that morning in the Massachusetts villages of Concord and Lexington. From that day forward, the course of future events would be more certain—and far more dangerous.

Bells had rung up and down the valley early that afternoon, giving the Stark family its first indication that something out of the ordinary was happening. With his family clustered about him, John Stark stood in the doorway in his shirt sleeves, for it was a mild day. He listened attentively, identifying the individual bells. From Litchfield and Londonderry, Goffestown and Merrimack, and sounding across Pine Pitch Plain from Bedford, the bells joined in clanging chorus. Downriver a cannon boomed.

Molly Stark, standing beside her husband, looked at him anxiously. "What's the meaning?"

"It's a general alarm. It may be for fire, but I see no smoke."

"If not for fire, what then, Pa?" young Archie asked. "Is it trouble with the redcoats?"

"I don't know," his father answered honestly. "We'll not paint the devil on the wall till we know for certain."

"Who's to tell us?" Caleb asked.

"There'll be a rider along with the news," his father promised. "Till then, we'll stand firm."

The next two hours were frustrating for Caleb, as he watched neighboring farmers on horseback gallop north and south along the road, plainly uncertain of the direction they should take but eager to be on the move. Several of the horsemen reined in at the Stark farmhouse to recount wild rumors they had heard. "War has begun," they said. "The redcoats were in Dunstable—Pelham—New Salem. . . . Women and children are being butchered."

In the midst of these alarms and rumors, Caleb noted that his father did indeed stand firm, awaiting word that he could trust. Meanwhile, there was work to be done. When the bells had begun to ring, he had been cutting logs in his sawmill on the banks of the Merrimack, a short distance behind his house. He now took up this interrupted task. Not until midafternoon did he shut down the sawmill gate, when informed by Tom Pickett that a man he knew to be a trusted courier of the Sons of Liberty had come riding into the yard.

John Stark lost no time then. He ran to meet the weary rider. As they clasped hands, the rider leaned forward in his saddle. "It's come, Captain," he said hoarsely. "Our boys have met the lobsterbacks at Lexington and Concord. And now we're driving them back toward Boston. There's need of you there, with all the men you can gather."

John Stark nodded grimly. "I'm ready to leave. Has much blood been let?"

"Enough. More of their blood than ours, I hear." The rider wheeled his horse about. "God be with ye, Cap'n," he shouted over his shoulder, as he galloped off.

Molly Stark walked to her husband's side and silently handed him his musket, powder horn, and cartouche box. Tom Pickett led the Captain's horse from the stable. John Stark looked critically at his mount, checking girth and stirrups, making sure that saddlebags and blanket roll were secure. Then he nodded approvingly to Tom. "All's in readiness. You're a good hand, Tom. I'd like to have ye with me. But with your stiff leg, you'd best tend to the farm. I'll feel better, knowing you're here."

"I'll do my best," Tom gruffly replied.

John Stark turned to his wife. "There's food for the journey?"

"Two days' food supply in your saddlebags," Molly Stark assured him. She lifted his two young daughters toward him. Sarah and Elizabeth giggled with pleasure as he kissed them, and their chubby arms tightened about his neck. Next he shook hands with Archie. "Look after your ma," he ordered, "and do what she wants." It was plain to see that Archie was itching to be off with his father, but he nodded his compliance.

John Stark turned to Caleb. "With trouble brewing, you'll be needed back at Gramp's farm. Get there first thing tomorrow and give him a true account of what's transpired."

Caleb agreed. He too yearned to go with his pa, but— like Archie—he knew better than to make such a request. A few months from now he would be of age, and if there was fighting still to be done no one could say him nay. Meanwhile, he must bide his time.

John Stark kissed his wife lightly. "I'll miss ye, Mrs. Stark."

Molly Stark blinked back a tear. "You know I'll miss you. And do try to be careful."

How many times has she seen him off to war? Caleb wondered, as his father mounted up. War and hardship, he suddenly realized, had been his parents' lot since childhood.

"You know I'm a cautious man," John Stark said gravely, bending down toward his wife.

Molly gulped. "I know the opposite is true. That's why I worry." Impulsively she reached up and hugged her husband fiercely. "Come back soon, dear heart," she whispered.

They watched him depart then—out the farmyard, past the stile, and down the road. One final wave of his hand, and John Stark dug his heels into the horse's flanks. He was off to the war at a gallop, greatcoat ballooning out behind him, clods of mud flying from beneath his horse's hoofs.

Caleb learned later that his father reached Cambridge in four days, at the head of one thousand men. In every town and village through which he passed, men had flocked to ride into battle with this leader whose exploits during the French and Indian War were already a legend.

The fighting was all over when Stark and his men arrived at Cambridge, as the British had withdrawn across the narrow neck of land leading to Charlestown. The colonial troops knew it would be foolish to pursue them across Charlestown Neck, for this strip could be raked by the musket fire of British soldiers stationed on Bunker Hill and by the cannon of British ships of the line.

The troops assembled near this strategic strip of land at Cambridge, the home of Harvard College. And there, to the surprise of the British, the Americans settled down for a long wait, although next day British troops were ferried from the peninsula back to Boston. There was as yet no central direction of any consequence. This was the citizen army's own notion. It had chased the British so far. Now it would see what transpired. Harvard and the town of Cambridge, after weathering the initial shock of being suddenly invaded by several thousand amateur soldiers, rose nobly to the occasion. Space was provided in dormitories and private homes. The Harvard kitchen staff worked overtime preparing hot meals. Provisions were brought in from surrounding towns.

In the days that followed, Caleb heard conflicting stories of what had caused the first armed clash that was terminating in this long wait at Cambridge. Gradually he sorted out what he believed to be true. General Gage had sent a force of British regulars to catch a pair of rebel leaders, Sam

Adams and John Hancock, reported to be in Lexington. And Gage had ordered his troops, as part of the same operation, to confiscate a supply of cannon and ammunition that was concealed five miles beyond Lexington village, in Concord. This was part of England's new, harsher policy regarding confiscation of arms, believed to have been partially prompted by the King's anger when he learned of the assault on Fort William and Mary.

Caleb heard that Paul Revere, whom he had met at Major Sullivan's, had ridden to warn the residents of Concord and Lexington of the British intent, just as on that cold December day he had ridden to warn the men of the Portsmouth area. Revere had been captured by British troops, on this latest ride, and then released. But the British had retained his gallant little horse. It pained Caleb to think of this horse serving the redcoats. But Revere was safe. That was the main thing. And he had carried the alarm to Lexington.

When the redcoats had appeared in Lexington at dawn on the morning of April 19, they had been met by villagers drawn up on the green in military formation. There was an exchange of point-blank fire. Eight Americans had died and ten were wounded. With whoops and huzzas, the redcoats, who had sustained only one casualty in this initial encounter, pursued the fleeing villagers. The British had marched on to Concord, then, and had destroyed what few military stores they could find.

It had all seemed so easy. But then the regulars had been ordered to destroy the north bridge at Concord village. And that had been the turning point. The citizen soldiers had held fast. They had fired a volley, picking off half the British officers at the bridge, and the redcoats had retired in confusion.

All the way back to Boston they had marched, twenty-one nightmarish miles, with armed Minutemen shooting at them from behind trees and rocks. The British had marched out to Lexington to the tune of "Yankee Doodle," a song popular in both the British and American camps, but then, as one soldier put it, "We made them dance it back again." Only the arrival of fifteen hundred British reinforcements and two fieldpieces had saved the remnants of the British force.

Now the British had withdrawn to lick their wounds. And at Cambridge the citizen army waited patiently for the next act to begin. There his father waited. Caleb ached to be with him.

13

☆ ☆
☆

Reverend Pickels laced plump fingers over his corpulent stomach and leaned slightly forward to read from the well-thumbed Bible that lay open on the table before him. "The Gospel according to John, Chapter One, Verse One," he intoned in his rich voice. " 'In the beginning was the Word, and the Word was with God, and the Word was God. The same was in the beginning with God. All things were made by Him; and without Him was not any thing made that was made. . . .' "

Caleb loved the rolling cadence of these Bible passages, which Reverend Pickels read as a regular part of their weekly study sessions, conducted in Captain Page's parlor. But on this balmy day in the second week of June, Caleb found his attention wandering. There were chores aplenty that needed doing, and Caleb knew that if he had belonged to almost any other farm household in Dunbarton he would spend this day working. But Gramp was prosperous enough to encourage learning in his household. Caleb considered this a mixed blessing.

Glancing down the long table, he saw that his Cousin John and Zeb Snavely were paying little attention to the pastor's words. Not that they ever did pay really close attention, Caleb thought, for he knew that Cousin John attended these sessions only because of Uncle Bill's insistence. And Zeb persisted in his educational pursuits because they furnished his only excuse to observe the—it was hoped —treasonable activities in the Page household. Zeb remained his usual smiling, obsequious self, and although Caleb avoided him as much as possible he was forced to go along with Gramp's judgment that it was best to avoid an open break with near neighbors.

Caleb's wandering thoughts were jolted back to the study session as he heard Reverend Pickels address him by name. "What do you think that passage means, my boy?"

"Why, I think it means God was present before the earth and the heavens," Caleb answered quickly. "His spirit endures forever."

Reverend Pickels' plump face broadened into a smile. "Well said. And I thought I had lost your attention." He looked sharply at Zeb and Cousin John. "I doubt that either of you could have answered as well, for you've both been mooning and glooming this whole morning." He sighed. "I should expect it, for on a day in spring youth seeks more sprightly pursuits than the dull quest for knowledge." He glanced at an unopened volume next to the Bible. "I was about to read from Pope's *Essay on Man*, but I see it will be a waste." He waved a pudgy hand. "Be off, then. And next week, for your cyphering class, complete the two problems I've written in your sum books."

Cousin John quickly gathered together his papers, quill pen, ink bottle, and book. "Thank you, sir," he said, bobbing his head. "I'll have the sums ready." Turning quickly toward the entrance to the front hallway, he nearly collided with Captain Page, who was about to enter the room.

"Steady, lad," Gramp cautioned, as he backed off a step.

"Pardon, Cap'n," Cousin John apologized, dashing for the front entrance.

"Don't slam the door!" Gramp shouted after him. He winced as the front door slammed behind Cousin John.

Zeb smiled engagingly at Caleb's grandfather. "Morning, Cap'n. A fine day."

Gramp mumbled a greeting to Zeb. He didn't pretend to be overly friendly with the Snavelys.

"Your study period's a short one," Gramp said, as he walked behind the long table and seated himself next to Reverend Pickels.

"I can't hold their attention," the cleric admitted. "There's spring in the air."

"That reminds me," Gramp said to Caleb. "Young Pru Davis brought over some gingerbread from her ma. She's in the kitchen. Says she wants to help Angie with her cooking." He winked. "Seems to me, she's really bent on seeing you."

Caleb hesitated. He had no desire to leave the men alone with Zeb, for he knew that the two old cronies talked freely, after the fashion of New Hampshiremen who have lived a free life and possess a clear conscience. Zeb evidently was in no hurry to depart. He remained sitting at the table, presumably studying his sums. But Caleb knew he had his ears cocked for any choice information he might acquire in this rebel household.

"Go on, go on," Gramp said impatiently to Caleb. "It's not every day such a pretty girl comes calling."

Caleb left reluctantly. He found Prudence at the kitchen hearth, her face flushed from the heat as she stirred Injun meal mixed with water in an iron pot, a mixture that would eventually become hasty pudding.

Pru favored Caleb with a welcoming smile. "Lands, Caleb," she exclaimed, stirring vigorously, "what are you doing out in the kitchen?"

"Gramp said for me to come out and see you," Caleb explained, with complete honesty.

The long wooden stirring spoon moved more slowly. "Why would he say a thing like that?"

Caleb shrugged. "Dunno." Suddenly he grinned. "Might be so I could see how pretty you look."

Pru's face flushed a deeper pink, and the stirring spoon moved faster. "It's just an old calico dress I'm wearing," she said breathlessly. She smiled over her shoulder at Caleb. "But I'm glad you think it's pretty."

Caleb also blushed. "I dunno about your dress," he said in a low voice. "It's you I think is pretty." Abruptly he took the stirring spoon from her hand and placed it beside the pot. "That's stirred enough. Come on outside, where it's cooler."

"It has warmed up some," Pru agreed, as she followed Caleb to a bench outside the door. They sat stiffly, side by side.

"Your folks good?" Caleb asked.

Pru nodded. "How's yours?"

"All right, last I heard. Pa's down country, you know. He's got himself a colonel's commission, and he's heading up all the New Hampshire troops in Massachusetts Bay. I hear they're stationed at Medford. That's near Charlestown Neck."

Pru's eyes grew large. "A colonel! Your pa's doing real good, Caleb. Don't you wish you were with him?"

"Don't I just! But Gramp won't hear of it. You know how he is about me going off to war. And I'm not of age yet to do as I will."

"War's a terrible hard thing sometimes," Pru said. "Didn't you find it so when you took the powder from that fort off New Castle?"

"You couldn't call that war," Caleb protested. "That was like taking a piece of pie. But this thing my pa's in— this is the real thing." There was a rising note of excitement in his voice. "There's big doings afoot. In that Second Continental Congress in Philadelphia, every colony's offering help to form a real army. And up on Lake Champlain last month, Ethan Ellen and his Green Mountain Boys, along with that cocky Benedict Arnold—they showed the British who was boss. Caught the commanding officer in bed and took Fort Ti away from 'em, by thunder."

"Even so," Pru stubbornly insisted, "what you did was of real help, too. That powder you took from the fort is being sent to help your pa's troops. They're real short of powder down there."

Caleb gave the girl his full attention. "How do you know? I hadn't heard that."

"Your hired girl, Angie, told me."

"Who told Angie?"

Pru wrinkled her nose. "I never heard so many questions. Angie said she heard Reverend Pickels telling Granny Page this morning."

"Did he tell Gramp too?"

"I declare," Pru protested, "you'd think I was on trial. No, of course he couldn't tell him. You know Captain Page just got back from town."

Caleb groaned. "Then he's probably in the front room right now, giving Gramp the news."

"What's the harm in that?"

"What's the harm?" Caleb demanded. "Zeb's there! That's the harm! It's what you might call a calamity!"

Caleb dashed into the house, leaving Pru sitting on the bench. He raced toward the closed door to the sitting room but deliberately slowed his pace as he approached. It wouldn't do to appear disturbed, he told himself, as he slicked down his hair with the flat of his hand. He took a deep breath and entered the room, deliberately slamming the door behind him.

This had the desired effect of stopping conversation. Reverend Pickels and Gramp both regarded him coldly. Caleb, looking around the room and seeing no sign of Zeb, felt a quick sense of relief.

"Back again, I hear," Gramp said mildly. "That was a brief courtship."

"Pru had to leave," Caleb said lamely. "I mean, I had to leave. What I mean to say is, we both had to leave."

Gramp narrowed his eyes. "When I was courting, my girl and I would both leave in the same direction. Howsoever, I don't pretend to understand the young'uns today." He turned to Reverend Pickels. "Now, what were you saying about that powder from the fort?"

Caleb tensed. "You been talking about the powder, Reverend?" he interrupted.

Reverend Pickels looked annoyed. "I was about to. Yes."

"Did you speak of the powder while Zeb was in the room?" Caleb persisted.

"You think me a fool?" the pastor demanded. He inclined his head toward a closed door leading from the sitting room to a hallway that served as a side entrance. "Zeb took his leave a while back, out that way, before we discussed such matters."

Caleb looked suspiciously toward the door. "But you have been talking about taking the powder to the troops. Did ye discuss its location?"

"I was about to—if you'll let me fit a word in edgewise. Now I've forgot what I was saying."

"You said the greater portion of the powder's stored in Madbury," Gramp prompted.

"So I did. At Captain Demeritt's house." Reverend Pickels paused, mouth open, as Caleb raised a hand in a peremptory demand for silence.

Both his grandfather and Reverend Pickels looked annoyed but resisted the impulse to speak, as Caleb tiptoed quietly to the closed side door. He had detected a barely audible rustling noise outside. Caleb threw open the door —and Zeb nearly tumbled into the room. Just as Caleb had suspected, Zeb had been crouched on the other side of the panel with his ear against the wood. Zeb blinked up at him, his face a fiery red, and then abruptly began crawling around the hallway floor on hands and knees. "Lost my pen," he explained in a tight voice. "I'm hunting for my pen."

"It's in your pocket," Caleb coldly informed him, pointing to a long quill projecting from the boy's jacket.

Zeb leaped to his feet. "So it is. No need to hunt further." With two long strides, he was at the side door, and in another instant he was out of the house and hurrying across the yard.

Reverend Pickels gasped. "Well, I never!"

Gramp's eyes flashed. "The insolence of that pup! To have the privacy of my own home violated—"

"He was in a good position to hear your every word," Caleb said, deeply concerned. "What's to do now?"

"There's naught to do, that I can see," Gramp answered. "The Reverend spoke only of things that are common knowledge hereabout."

"Common knowledge perhaps to the Sons of Liberty," Reverend Pickels said slowly, "but are we sure the Tories are so well informed?"

"I'd say not," Caleb answered promptly. "Not when Zeb will take such a risk to spy upon us. If I don't miss my guess, he now has some choice news to feed the King-lovers around Portsmouth."

Reverend Pickels nodded his agreement. "Especially those loyalists in the Madbury area. They'd dearly love to learn of Captain Demeritt's trip to the troops at Medford with an oxcart of powder."

"I fear they will learn of it," Caleb said. "Either Zeb or his pa will make sure of that."

"We put too much importance on this matter," Captain Page said impatiently. "You think they'll ride the long road to the seacoast with news of such small import?"

"I do indeed," Caleb replied. He took a deep breath. "And I think it's up to us to tell Captain Demeritt what's in the wind."

His grandfather looked at him shrewdly. "When you say 'us,' lad, you're talking about yourself. I know how badly you yearn to join the action. And here's a ready-made excuse. Confess now, Caleb, is that how your thoughts run?"

Caleb kept his temper in check. In a tightly controlled voice he said, "I think only that Captain Demeritt must be warned. Someone must carry the word, and I'm willing to go."

"And I'm not willing to *have* ye go," the old Captain said in a voice suddenly choked with emotion. "Let that be an end to it."

Caleb remained silent, realizing that further talk with his grandfather would serve no purpose. Caleb knew that Gramp couldn't bear to see him go riding off, probably to be pulled into this conflict, just as Gramp's only son had ridden off to an earlier war and never returned. Caleb could appreciate the depth of his feelings. But what of his pa's soldiers, whose safety depended on the safe arrival of the gunpowder? And Captain Demeritt probably was not aware that British sympathizers knew of his plans.

Caleb's teeth clenched tight. He wanted so desperately to be off that his yearning was almost a physical hurt.

14

Caleb slept fitfully that night. Shortly before dawn he heard galloping hoofbeats in the distance, but his sleep-fogged consciousness did not immediately respond. Pounding hoofs had been part of his dreams that entire night, as his dream self had ridden a great black stallion on seemingly endless missions to warn shadowy figures of approaching danger. Now, as the sharp clop of hoofs on dirt drew nearer, Caleb came fully awake with a start. He ran to his bedroom window and looked out on the road.

In the pre-dawn haze he saw a horseman riding down the road from the direction of the Snavely farm. Caleb strained forward, his nose pressed tight against the pane, as the figure on horseback rode past a gate leading to the Page farm. Caleb felt a rising sense of excitement. Although it was difficult to be certain in this dim light, he was fairly sure that the rider was Zeb. If only he would turn his head! The next moment, as if on cue, the rider did look toward the house, his face inclined toward Caleb's window.

Caleb saw a flash of white teeth, and then the horseman was gone down the road. It was Zeb—and laughing at me! Caleb thought. He was fully awake, now, and hopping mad. Zeb was off to tell the loyalists of Demeritt's plan to take powder to the troops. No question of that. And no question now in Caleb's mind about his own course of action. He must ride to warn Captain Demeritt.

As he quickly dressed, Caleb's mind raced ahead to details of the preparations he must make for his trip. He would saddle the sure-footed roan mare that Gramp had given him. He must take powder, ball, and extra flints along with his musket; some journeycake and parched corn to eat on the way; an extra shirt and socks. That was all. He would travel light.

He decided against leaving a message for Gramp. What was there to say? They had been over and over the same ground so often. Perhaps in time Gramp would understand and forgive. Caleb hoped so. But such considerations must not weaken his resolution to take off after Zeb as quickly as possible.

A half hour later he was on the road, reining in his frisky mare. There was a long ride ahead, and his mount must settle down to a steady pace. Behind him, Caleb had left a sleeping household. Ahead lay a narrow ford over the Merrimack River above Hooksett Falls and then the daylong journey eastward to Madbury, just north of Durham.

If circumstances had been different, it would have been a pleasant journey. The day turned warm, and at intervals the sun shone brightly on Caleb as he traveled past open fields; at other times, the sun spread dappled patterns, filtering through foliage that arched over long stretches of the road. Yet Caleb was scarcely aware of the day's charm. His whole attention was concentrated on the road ahead.

Zeb was riding somewhere along that road. Caleb could easily follow the fresh hoofmarks of Zeb's horse in the dirt road. If Zeb should stop to eat or rest, Caleb felt that he would overtake him. He fingered his musket, knowing that he must make an effort to stop Zeb if he came within range. But the thought made him uneasy. No matter what their differences might be, the fact remained that he had grown up with Zeb as a near neighbor. Could he point a gun at Zeb, with intent to kill? To his surprise, Caleb found that he was unconsciously pulling back on the reins, slowing his mount. It was obvious that he really did not want to meet Zeb. Caleb clenched his teeth and slapped his horse on the flank. An end to this shilly-shallying. If they were fated to meet, so be it.

He rode through Deerfield and into Nottingham. More than halfway there now, with the sun high in a blue sky. But he knew that the mare was tiring. His own stomach growled a request for food. Finally Caleb rested beside a small stream. Unless Zeb too was pausing to rest, there was small chance of catching him now. But that could not be helped. This rest was necessary. Never before had journey-cake tasted so good.

Caleb reached Madbury in late afternoon. He had long since lost sight of the hoofmarks made by Zeb's horse, for the closer he came to the Great Bay area the more traffic he met. Wagons, oxcarts, horsemen, and men on foot traveled the dusty road. From one of the foot travelers, Caleb learned that Captan Demeritt's farm was a mile farther up the road at Hick's Hill.

"The Captain's there right now," he was told by a chunky young man in work clothes. "He's been powerful busy of late, and some of us been lending a hand." The young man had gazed at Caleb with unconcealed curiosity. "You fixing to lend him a hand?"

"I just might," Caleb replied.

But when Caleb reached the Captain's large farmhouse and tied his horse to a hitching post near the side porch, he received the definite impression that his help was not wanted. Three workmen, coming in from the field, favored him with suspicious glances and walked quickly away as he called to them. Nobody answered his knock at the kitchen door. Not until Caleb started walking toward the barn did he receive any attention. Halfway there, he was stopped by a boy about twelve years old, who came running from the barn and stood directly in his path.

"What's your business?" the boy asked belligerently.

This rude reception angered Caleb. After all, he had left his comfortable home, perhaps for good and all, had spent a hard day in the saddle, and had risked an armed encounter, all to carry a warning to this inhospitable place. He scowled at the boy. "My business is my business, young fella. I want the whereabouts of Captain Demeritt."

The youngster returned his scowl. "The Captain's whereabouts are his business and none of yours."

Caleb could stand no more of this. He grasped the boy firmly by the shoulder and squeezed hard. "You listen here—" he began.

"Pa!" the boy screamed in a high, shrill voice. "He's hurting me!"

The next moment a tall, long-legged man came running from the barn. He was dressed in the striped blue-and-white cotton work frock worn by many farmers, which buttoned high at the neck and extended to just above his knees. Although his smock limited the farmer's stride somewhat, Caleb noticed that he was bearing down on him with alarming speed. Caleb quickly released the boy, who immediately attempted to kick him in the shins. Holding him at arm's length, Caleb divided his attention between this immediate threat and the oncoming farmer.

"Leave off!" the farmer shouted, as he came to a halt just behind the lad. Grasping his son's collar, he pulled him away from Caleb.

"Watch him, Pa," the boy panted. "He's a mean one!"

The farmer clapped his big hands. "Be off!" he ordered the boy.

The youngster hesitated for a moment, took one look at his father's face, and decided to comply. He walked off slowly, glancing back over his shoulder, unwilling to miss any of the expected excitement.

The farmer's level gray eyes looked searchingly at Caleb. "My boy thinks you a mean one. Are ye?"

"I could say the same about your boy," Caleb replied in a voice that he tried to keep calm.

The farmer nodded. "So ye could. Did he kick ye?"

"No," Caleb replied in a tight voice, "though he tried hard enough."

"It's a bad habit the lad has," the farmer admitted. "He's even booted me a time or two. But I kick him back. It gives him cause for reflection." Suddenly the farmer's face broke into a wide smile. "But I'll admit it's no way to greet visitors. Ye must think we're all daft hereabouts. We are in fact what ye might call a wee bit edgy." He extended his hand. "I'm John Dermeritt."

Caleb sighed. "At long last. I've come a far road to your door, Captain." He shook the farmer's hand. "I'm Caleb Stark."

Dermeritt continued to grasp Caleb's hand as he bent forward and peered closely at his face. "Say ye so. You'd be John Stark's boy then."

"The very same," Caleb assured him.

Abruptly Demeritt released Caleb's hand and flung an arm about his shoulder. "Of course. I was trying to remember where I'd seen ye before. 'Twas at the time we stormed the fort off New Castle. What can I do for ye?"

A slow grin crossed Caleb's face. "I'm trying to do something for you, if you'll let me."

Demeritt looked abashed. "What is it you're trying to say, lad?"

Caleb told him of the news they had heard in Dunbarton concerning an expected shipment of gunpowder to the troops at Medford.

"You heard right," the Captain agreed. "The troops are so hard pressed for gunpowder, it's pitiful." He lowered his voice. "Ye recall the powder we took from the fort? Part of it was hid beneath the pulpit at Durham. Some of that's been brought here to my farm. And now in the barn there's an oxcart we're loading with twenty barrels of powder for your pa's troops. Truth to tell, that's why we're so edgy today. It's a risky business."

"And likely to grow more risky," Caleb added. "Did ye know the loyalists are aware of your plan?"

That was a possibility, Demeritt admitted, although he

had tried to keep his plan quiet. "Old General 'Granny' Gage has his King-lovers well posted," he said. "They seem to be on to our every move."

"There's one made a special trip this day to make sure the loyalists are alerted," Caleb said. He told of following Zeb, and of his failure to overtake him.

"That makes it certain then," Demeritt said. His bushy eyebrows drew together in a scowl. "But they'll not stop us. Tomorrow we start our journey to Medford, and that powder will get to the troops."

Caleb's eyes brightened. "Let me ride guard."

"I dunno about that," Demeritt said doubtfully. "I know you to be a good lad, but nonetheless, if harm befalls ye, I'm to blame."

"But I'll be heading your way in any event," Caleb pleaded. "My plan was, after bringing word to you, to journey on to Medford and ask Pa's permission to sign on with his troops. I may be only fifteen, but—"

The Captain stopped him. "You're sixteen, ye say? Well, that puts things in a different light. A lad sixteen is a man grown and can do as he likes. I'd have no objection to a man of sixteen accompanying the powder cart."

Caleb was puzzled. "I guess you didn't hear aright. I said—" He paused as Demeritt's words finally made sense to him. "Yes, sir," he said meekly. "You'll have no trouble with a steady man such as me at your side."

"And how old did ye tell me you are?" the Captain demanded.

Caleb gulped. "Sixteen."

The Captain nodded. "I'll take your word for it, for you're a lad who's good and trustworthy."

"And conniving," Caleb added.

Dermeritt winked. "I'm the conniver. I fear you'll learn bad habits if ye travel with me. But at least the trip will not be dull."

) 138 (

Caleb's heart beat faster. Tomorrow couldn't come fast enough to suit him.

15

"Does it look like a load of hay?" Captain Demeritt asked Caleb the next morning, as they stood in the barn, inspecting a farm cart hitched to a yoked team of oxen.

"It does to me," Caleb replied. This was his first view of the powder cart—a low-slung affair, riding on two large, spoked wheels at its center. The wheel rims reached almost to the top of three-foot hemlock stakes that were secured at intervals around the edge of the cart. There were five stakes on each side and two at each end, all tied together with connecting ropes, so that they formed an enclosure for what appeared to be a heaping hay pile.

"There's twenty barrels of powder beneath that sprinkling of hay," Demeritt said. "A combustible load." He grinned at Caleb. "How would ye like to travel atop of it?"

"Perhaps they're the selfsame barrels that furnished me a seat in the gundalow," Caleb reminded him.

"Let's hope your good fortune continues this trip," the Captain replied.

They turned toward the barn door as two men in farm clothing entered. Caleb greeted the men, as Demeritt had made a point of having him meet them last evening, before Caleb had bedded down for the night in the Demeritts' spare bedroom; they were neighboring farmers who had volunteered to help take the powder to Medford. Fred

Baldwin, the older of the two, was a squat, slow-speaking man. His companion, Ira Nearing, was tall and angular, with sharp features and nervous mannerisms. Each carried a musket, powder horn, and bullet pouch.

Ira looked admiringly at the cart. "Done a good job. Good job, John. Good job," he said in his quick, jerky way of speaking.

Demeritt looked pleased. "Thank ye, Ira. I think it's good enough to fool some of our loyalists busybodies."

Fred Baldwin puffed on a stubby pipe. "I'll take one last drag on this," he said. "I dare not smoke near the powder."

"If ye like," the Captain offered, "you can walk the first lap of the way alongside the oxen. That way ye can smoke like a chimney and no harm done." He turned to Caleb. "The way I figure it, we'll have two men riding atop the load and two men walking. Then we can change off from time to time. It's going to be a long trip down country anyway—at least sixty miles."

"I'll walk. Walk with Fred," Ira volunteered. "I get that nervous on a trip. Have to be doing. Up and doing."

"Well, Caleb," Dermeritt said, "I guess that puts you and me atop the cart, at least for the first few miles."

"I'll collect my duds and be right along," Caleb promised. He looked toward a stall at the rear of the barn. "First off, I'd like to look after my mare."

"As you will," the Captain said, "but she's in good hands. My boy Johnny's looking after her."

Caleb was startled. "You mean the boy who tried to kick my shins?"

"The same. He felt real bad about trying to kick you, when he found you'd come here to help. He put a curry-comb to your mare first thing this morning."

"Johnny's a good boy. Good boy," Ira assured Caleb. "Hot head maybe. But good heart. That boy's got a real good heart."

Caleb had to admit, as he inspected his horse, that she did look well cared for. Her coat gleamed. Her mane and tail were well brushed. And the stall contained clean hay. The boy evidently could do a job when he put his mind to it. Caleb prolonged his inspection longer than was necessary, for he was reluctant to leave his one last link with home. At length he turned away and almost tripped over young Johnny Demeritt, who was standing directly behind him. The boy looked up wordlessly at Caleb.

"What are you trying to do now? Break my leg?" Caleb inquired. But a broad smile belied the harshness of his words.

Johnny slowly returned the smile. "How's she look?"

"Wonderful," Caleb answered. "It would do her good, while I'm away, for her to have some exercise. Would ye care to ride her?"

The boy beamed. "Ride her? Of, yes! Thank you!"

"Thank *you*," Caleb said gravely. He was leaving his horse in good hands, he knew, and that was a weight off his mind. Now it was time to prepare for his trip.

"Good luck," the boy called as Caleb walked away.

Caleb waved to him. He had a feeling he'd need all the good fortune he could gather for this journey.

The four travelers started off within the hour. We look an innocent-enough party, Caleb thought, although the oxen are straining to pull so light a load. He sat high upon the load of hay, next to Demeritt. It was a hard seat, for the hay barely covered the barrels of gunpowder. They kept their muskets concealed beneath the hay at their feet, together with the muskets of the two farmers who walked beside the oxen. Dermeritt had decided that it would look unnatural if these two carried muskets in addition to the switches they used to encourage the ox team. Caleb doubted the wisdom of this move, as the loyalists who were aware of the true contents of their cart would not be fooled by Ira and Fred's harmless appearance. He wisely kept his own counsel, however, and maintained a careful watch on the road ahead.

They had traveled two miles down the winding country road when Ira suddenly called a halt. He pointed ahead to a wooden area where several crows cawed loudly as they circled tall pine trees. Other crows perched in the pines, making a fearful racket. "Heed the crows," Ira sputtered. "What's amiss up ahead? Crows know. Heed them now."

Quickly the Captain handed muskets to the two men on foot. He and Caleb each took their own muskets from the hay and looked to the priming. Ira switched the near ox, and the team plodded forward. Docile, unimaginative beasts, Caleb thought. So they would move unswervingly forward to the very gates of Hades. He himself, leaning tensely forward on his high perch, did not possess such a temperament. Nor did his companions, judging by their tense, anxious expressions. All expected a trap waiting to be closed on them near the pines, and all were ready for instant action.

They found a dead dog, horribly mangled, lying in the road under the pines. This was the cause of the crows' excited chatter. Ira laughed self-consciously as he handed back his musket to Caleb. "Crow talk! Feast or warning. Sounds the same to me."

They were all smiling now, relieved that the imagined crisis had passed. A clear road lay ahead. A peaceful land-scape of rolling green fields stretched away on either side—like a patchwork quilt, Caleb thought, with stone walls for stitching.

When danger did come, it caught them unaware. The cart was passing down a narrow stretch of road bordered by large maple trees. If Caleb had been looking up, he thought afterward, he would have seen the two men, par-tially concealed in the foliage, crouched on thick maple limbs that overhung the road. As it was, the first indication that Caleb had of their presence was the glimpse of a shadowy form hurtling down upon him. Caleb shouted a warning, as the figure landed on him with a bone-jarring thump. At the same time another man jumped from the tree and landed square on Demeritt's shoulders, toppling both the Captain and his assailant over the side of the cart. Two more men rushed from behind trees and leaped on Ira and Fred, who fought fiercely to defend themselves, as the oxen stopped stockstill and calmly waited for further commands.

Caleb toppled backward in the cart, scattering the thin covering of hay that had camouflaged the powder barrels. He rolled over onto them as his attacker's strong arms twined about his chest with a force that threatened to crack Caleb's ribs. A sudden desperate twist momentarily broke the grip, and Caleb lunged toward the muskets at the front of the cart. His groping hand was caught in a viselike grip before he could grasp his musket. The next moment his assailant was standing, teetering on the barrels' rounded surfaces and pulling Caleb up beside him. Caleb stifled a cry of pain as the stocky, hairy individual spun him about and twisted his arm behind him. From the merciless, unyielding pressure that was being exerted, Caleb knew that the man intended to break his arm. Quickly bending down and away, Caleb threw the hairy one off balance for a moment and then smashed the back of his head against the man's face. Caleb felt a stinging sensation and a momentary dizziness as his head made thudding contact. He knew that he must have a scalp wound, but his maneuver made the fellow momentarily loosen his grip on Caleb's arm. Quickly Caleb spun away from him and, wheeling about, drove his fist hard into his assailant's already bruised and bloody face. A tooth flew out as the man staggered backward against the lines laced around stakes at the edge of the cart. Another blow tipped him backward over the waist-high rope. As he crashed onto the dusty road, Caleb leaped down beside him, pulled him to his feet, and hit him solidly on the jaw. The hairy one dropped heavily to the ground and lay still.

Massaging his skinned knuckles, Caleb for the first time had an opportunity to look about him and see how his friends were faring. Demeritt seemed to be holding his own against a bull-necked individual who had the build of a wrestler but was being held off by the Captain's well-aimed blows. Ira and Fred also were doing well. Fred was matched against an older man, who seemed to be losing his enthusiasm for this contest. Ira's foe was a wiry lad in his late teens. Ira, although still full of fight, was breathing hard.

Caleb suddenly remembered his musket in the cart. That would put an end to this affair in short order. It was a wonder to him that the men who had ambushed the cart had not carried guns. They probably didn't dare risk the sound of a shot. That certainly would have alerted the surrounding countryside, where almost every farmer was a Minuteman.

Caleb turned toward the cart, but the thought of securing his musket was driven abruptly from his mind by sight of a black powder trail extending from an open barrel lying on the road beneath the rear of the cart. The barrel was easily seen, for it had been pushed only about two feet underneath the cart. As Caleb's gaze followed the trail twenty yards down the road behind the cart, his eyes opened wide. There was a lad kneeling at the end of the powder trail who resembled Zeb. Caleb looked closely, and there was no doubt in his mind. It *was* Zeb! And evidently he was playing an important role in this attack. While Zeb's confederates were battling with Caleb and his friends, Zeb must have broken open a powder barrel and spread a trail of the deadly black stuff from the cart to the position he now held.

Caleb raced forward to stop Zeb, who was frantically striking flint on steel in an attempt to make a spark that would ignite the powder. Caleb was ten yards from his goal when Zeb's frenzied efforts finally did produce a spark. In an instant the hissing, smoking powder train was burning toward Caleb. He made an abrupt about-face. He must get to that open powder barrel beneath the cart and kick it out of the way. The next moment he was borne to the ground as Zeb ran up behind him and leaped on his back. Desperately, Caleb reached out with his foot, attempting to break the powder train at his side before it ignited. But Zeb held him back.

"Scatter!" Zeb cried. His fellows must have been waiting for this signal, for they shook off their opponents immediately and raced for a gully at the roadside. Even the hairy one that Caleb had beaten rose groggily to his feet and staggered toward safety.

"Watch the powder! It's going up!" Caleb shouted to his friends, who, unexpectedly released from combat, were staring about them in a puzzled way. His cry roused them to action, and they too plunged over the bank.

Sheer desperation gave Caleb the extra strength he needed to break loose from Zeb. And then he was running, faster than he had ever run before—racing toward the powder barrel.

Now the ignited power train was only a few inches from the barrel. I'll never make it! Caleb thought despairingly. He must have been more tired than he realized. His lungs felt as if they would burst. But somewhere within himself he found the strength for one final burst of speed. His foot kicked the barrel. It rolled toward the gully, and the smoking powder train fizzled out at the spot where, a second before, it would have triggered a tremendous explosion.

Caleb sat down weakly on a hummock at the roadside, as Demeritt, with Ira and Fred, rushed from the gully and snatched their muskets from the cart. A warning shot fired over Zeb's head, as he tried to run away, effectively changed his mind. He returned slowly to the cart. Two shots fired into the gully convinced his three cohorts to surrender.

By the time a group of farmers, alerted by the musket reports, had gathered from neighboring farms, Demeritt could report that matters were well in hand.

The four prisoners were tied with lengths of rope removed from the cart. They would be spending the next few days with a local farmer, who offered to keep the quartet out of circulation until he was sure the mission was completed. The powder was safe. And, barring a few cuts and bruises, all members of the Captain's party were in satisfactory condition.

"We're ready to be on our way," the Captain announced, "but this time we'll keep muskets at the ready."

Caleb walked over to Zeb, who stood staring at the ground. Zeb's arms were tied behind him. "I'm sorry to leave ye like this," Caleb told him. "I suppose I should forgive and forget. But when I think how you tried to blow us all to smithereens, I find it hard to do either."

Zeb raised his head and glared at Caleb. "I ask naught of you. Get on your way and leave me be."

Caleb looked at him for a long moment. "So be it. At least we know now where we stand. There's no more need for you to pretend friendship with Gramp's household."

Zeb spat on the ground. "That for you and your family!"

Caleb turned quickly away. Suddenly he could take no more of Zeb. He was tired, bone tired. And the journey had just begun.

16

It fretted Caleb to spend the night of June 16 at a farm-house north of Stoneham. He estimated that they were only about eight miles from their destination at Winter Hill, and he was anxious to complete their journey. His companions, however, were tired after their tedious trip behind plodding oxen from sunup to sundown each long summer day. An overnight stop at the home of a trusted leader in the Sons of Liberty was welcome.

Relaxing that evening on the farmhouse porch, after a hearty dinner, Caleb felt some of his tension drain away. Talk between his three companions and the farmer, Tom Law, made little impression on him, as he was deep in his own thoughts. He was considering how his father would react to his unexpected arrival in camp when suddenly he was jarred to full awareness of the conversation by Ira's excited exclamation. "Let 'em attack! I'll git me a lobster-back! Just in time we are. Just in time, I'd say. Ye think they'll dare attack?"

Caleb concentrated his full attention on Tom Law's grave reply. "I know they'll dare. The redcoats are that anxious to bust out of Boston, they're itching for action. It galls them, being hemmed in by our boys, with no means of supply save by sea."

Demeritt frowned. "How can ye know this for a fact?"

"We have our means of finding out what's brewing in their camp," the farmer replied. He told them of the situation as it existed around Boston. Understandably, due to his position in the Sons of Liberty, he seemed to possess a thorough understanding of the military situation. He spoke of the large American force—some put the figure as high as fifteen thousand men—camped in a nine-mile semicircle rimming Boston from Roxbury on the south, through Cambridge in the center, to Medford on the north. "That's where your pa has the largest single regiment in the entire army," Law told Caleb. "He's camped in the Winter Hill section of Medford with eight hundred men, and a mile away from him there's a smaller New Hampshire regiment under Jim Reed, stationed near Charlestown Neck."

Tom Law didn't think that the British force in Boston numbered more than five thousand, but among them were some of Britain's best troops. They were commanded by three famous generals, who had arrived last month from England to strengthen the hand of General Gage. The King, according to reports, made no secret of the fact that he considered Gage too timid; the new commanders would adopt a firmer policy toward the upstart rebel farmers. There was Major General William Howe, a hero of the French and Indian War, who had played a leading role in defeating the French at Quebec. He was a member of Parliament from a famed military family. Major General Henry Clinton, though a paunchy man with the face of a benign schoolmaster, was reputed to have a keen military mind. And, of course, there was Major General "Gentleman Johnny" Burgoyne, also a member of Parliament and a well-known playwright in England. When he had docked in Boston Harbor, he had promised his men, "We'll soon have elbow room."

"They're up to something big in Boston," Tom Law said gravely. "I've heard tell they plan to flank our position in a day or two and break through to our headquarters in Cambridge."

"What can we do to stop 'em?" Caleb demanded.

Tom Law winked at him. "With a man such as your pa on the scene, I wouldn't worry too much. There's some say we're planning to get the jump on 'em."

Demeritt leaned forward. "Would it be asking too much, Tom, for some idea on how we propose to do that?"

The farmer looked cautiously about him in the darkness and then also leaned forward. " 'Twill do no harm," he said in a hushed voice, "for I know you all to be men of honor. And you should know what you'll be heading toward tomorrow. Here then is the situation. The Charlestown peninsula is the key. If you look down on this peninsula from Copp's Hill in Boston, its appearance is like a thick, knobby war club that juts out between the Mystic River on its north side and the Charles River on its south. It tapers down to a small handle of land called Charlestown Neck that connects it with the mainland just below where two roads fork to Medford and Cambridge. On the peninsula, about a half mile from the Neck, is a sloping rise known as Bunker Hill. That's its highest point—about a hundred and ten feet. Then, farther on, there's a smaller rise, known variously as Breed's Hill or Charlestown Hill. South of that is the village of Charlestown, just across the Charles River from Boston. Most of the land outside the town grows to hay, for it's mainly pasture, divided by fences and stone walls."

Demeritt was growing impatient. "But what use is this land to us? Do we have need of pasture land?"

"We have need of this particular pasture land," the farmer replied, "before the British sail out from Boston to occupy it."

"That's their plan?"

"It is. If they can seize the peninsula, it will give them a strong base of operations—with their guns looking down the throats of our men across the Neck in Cambridge and Medford "

Fred Baldwin puffed on his stubby pipe. "I'd say it's up to our men to occupy the land first."

"From what I hear, that's just what we intend. In fact,"

Law added in a harsh whisper, "our boys may be digging in this very night, on either Bunker Hill or Breed's Hill."

Caleb's body tensed. "Then they'll have need of our powder. We should be traveling now, instead of talking."

"Relax, lad," his host said in a kindly voice. "Night travel's a chancy thing. Believe me, your powder will be just as welcome tomorrow."

Caleb slowly settled back in his chair. He yearned to be off, but Tom Law had impressed him with the scope of his knowledge. He had small choice but to rely on his word. He turned to Demeritt. "Then can we be away by first light?"

"Aye," Demeritt agreed. "I'm just as anxious to be off as you are."

"And me," Ira sputtered. "Me too. I'm that eager. Eager to go."

"I'll accompany your party, if I may," Law said. "It's my guess that every man able to shoulder a musket will soon be needed."

They started out next morning in the moist, fresh-smelling, pre-dawn hour. The lumbering oxen, refreshed by their night's rest, pulled with a will. Caleb and his four companions all walked, hoping to lighten the load so that the oxen would make maximum progress.

As the gray haze of early dawn lightened, Demeritt predicted that the day would be a fair one. The next moment, Caleb saw a glow that resembled heat lightning flicker in the hazy distance. This was followed by a low, ominous roll, sounding like distant thunder.

"Hate to dispute you," Caleb remarked, "but it looks to me like a storm's coming up."

Demeritt squinted anxiously ahead. "It's a storm, right enough," he said gruffly. "A man-made storm. Those are cannon."

Caleb gulped. Of course. He should have known. He'd

been close enough to the cannon's roar off Fort William and Mary.

Again there was a flicker of light on the horizon, followed by louder thunder. "Perhaps they're our cannon," Caleb said hopefully.

Tom Law shook his head. "No chance. The number of usable cannon we own, you could stick in your eye. I fear the bombardment is all incoming." He looked gravely at the Captain. "I think this means our lads may have dug in on the peninsula last night. The British probably have just caught sight of their positions."

"Then our powder's too late," Caleb burst out. "The battle's already begun!"

"Easy now," Demeritt urged. "There'll be plenty of use for our powder." He glanced toward the plodding oxen. "Though I do admit I too would prefer speedier transport."

Caleb wisely remained silent. Nothing he could do would quicken the oxen's pace. One mile. Two miles. Men were riding past them on horseback, spurring their mounts racing toward the Cambridge camp. Caleb longed to be astride one of those horses. But he would not leave this precious load of powder. He had come so far. He promised himself that he personally would deliver it to his pa's troops.

As they skirted Spot Pond, there was a momentary cessation of the distant thunder. It seemed unnaturally still to Caleb, as he looked over rolling fields now visible in the first rays of early morning sun. He wondered if the bombardment had ended.

A few minutes later, the entire horizon seemed to light up, the ground shook beneath their feet, and a blast of sound engulfed them. Demeritt jumped to the side of the near ox, steadying it as the beast rolled frightened eyes. Wave on wave of sound swept over them.

"The whole fleet's opened up!" Tom Law shouted. "Let's hope our boys are dug in deep!"

The bombardment continued sporadically for the rest of the trip. As they approached Medford in midmorning, Caleb breathed the acrid smell of powder. Now he could see red flashes and a pall of smoke in the east.

"Almost there now," Tom Law shouted to him, as they crossed a bridge leading from Medford village to an area that was swarming with men—some drilling on a broad parade, others sitting near small tents, many cleaning weapons. "Here's Winter Hill," Law told him. "This is your pa's regiment."

They halted the ox team, and Caleb looked about him. With a battle going on, he wondered what these men were doing here. He voiced his thought to Demeritt.

"This is the way it is in battle," Demeritt told him. "If *every* soldier crowded onto the peninsula, the British could close Charlestown Neck and have our boys in a bag. Your pa's probably holding the main line here, in case the redcoats manage to get this far."

It still didn't seem likely to Caleb that his father would relish such a role. He looked over the soldiers, hoping to find a familiar face. He'd take Tom Law's word that these were his pa's troops, but to his eyes they could be any group of farmers with muskets. He did see a couple of men wearing long swords, who seemed to be giving commands. Probably the swords meant that they were officers. Most of the men wore farm clothes, with their breeches fastened just below the knees, loose homespun coats and waistcoats, heavy wool stockings, and cowhide boots ornamented with large buckles. Their hats were mostly round and broad-brimmed, although some three-cornered hats were in evidence.

"Where's your pa?" Ira asked Caleb. "Let's see if we can find your pa. I'm that anxious. You must be too."

Now that the actual moment of meeting approached, Caleb didn't know if he was really that anxious to see his father. After all, he was a runaway. But, for better or worse, here he was. And, more important, here was the powder. "Where is he?" Caleb asked Law.

The farmer indicated a large residence up the street. "That's his headquarters, in the old Jonathan Wade house."

Captain Demeritt announced their arrival to one of a pair of guards outside the house. After bidding them wait, the guard disappeared inside the house, presumably in search of Colonel Stark. They struck up a conversation with the remaining guard, who seemed friendly and talkative. He confirmed Tom Law's surmise that the Americans had indeed dug in last night on the peninsula and built up earthworks to form a redoubt at the top of Breed's Hill. It was this exposed fort that now was drawing fire from the British warships *Somerset*, *Spitfire*, *Lively*, and *Falcon*, at anchor in the harbor. Solid balls, mixed with some explosive shells, also were being lobbed at the fort from the Copp's Hill gun battery in Boston.

"I hear our losses are light," the guard said. "Our fort's solidly built, with six-foot-high walls."

The Captain looked amazed. "And built in one night? It's a miracle!"

The dry voice of John Stark interrupted, as the Colonel walked from the house and approached the group. "If you call hard, backbreaking work a miracle, friend Demeritt, then that is what it is."

Demeritt quickly advanced toward Stark and grasped his outstretched hand. "John! I'm that glad to see ye!" He nodded toward the oxcart, where the barrels of powder now lay in plain sight. "We've brought a little present."

Stark's grim face relaxed as he regarded the powder. "Never have I seen a prettier sight. We're low, mighty low. And that's a fact." He turned his attention to the group standing with the Captain. "I thank you all." His gaze flickered over Caleb, but he gave no sign of recognition. Turning to Ira Nearing, he asked his name, and he made the same request of Fred Baldwin. Tom Law he seemed to know. Caleb uneasily met his father's ice-blue eyes, as they looked directly at him. "And who is this young man?" Stark asked.

Anger surged through Caleb, but he held himself in check. If his pa wanted to play games, he could play too. "Caleb Stark, sir," he said, in a voice that shook a little, in spite of himself.

His father pretended to be surprised. "Say ye so? There is a likeness, I'll admit. But I know for a fact you're not Caleb Stark"—Caleb bit his lip as his father continued—"for the boy I know by that name gave his word to stay in Dunbarton and help his grandfather."

This was more than Caleb could bear. "I had to come," he said hoarsely. "If ye don't want me here, just say the word. But don't torment me." He stood unflinching before his father, although the Colonel's eyes blazed and his fists clenched.

Quickly Demeritt stepped forward. "It's not my practice to interfere in family affairs, but you should know, John, that your boy traveled to my farm in Madbury to give me warning. He'd heard that we would be waylaid on the way down here with your powder."

"And were you?"

"We were. If it hadn't been for Caleb, the powder—and all of us with it—might have blown sky high." He explained Caleb's role in the struggle, as Stark kept his level gaze fixed on the boy.

When Demeritt had finished his account, John Stark spoke quietly to Caleb. "Was this trip made with your Gramp's permission?"

"No," Caleb admitted in a low voice.

"You just ran off?"

Caleb nodded.

"What's to be done then?" his father inquired sadly. "The old man's been hurt. Nothing will change that. And here you are. So," he said, his voice suddenly brisk, "we'd best put you to some use."

Caleb's expression brightened, as his father placed a hand on his shoulder.

"You've done me a service—no denying that." John Stark's voice softened as he added, "And it *is* good to see ye. No denying that, either." Abruptly he turned away. "Now there's no more time to waste." He called to the nearest guard. "Please bring me Major McClary." So now it's *Major* McClary, Caleb thought. His old friends were rising fast in the military service.

Caleb grinned a few minutes later as he watched the hulking McClary bend forward to ease his six-foot-six-inch frame through the front door of the headquarters building. As he strode toward them, an answering smile broke upon McClary's quarried features. He inclined his shaggy head toward Caleb but paid strict attention to Colonel Stark, who began briskly giving him instructions.

"Providential arrival of powder," Caleb heard his father tell McClary. "It's just in time—though I've not yet received orders to send reinforcements over the Neck. See that each man's given at least a gill of powder."

"I'll make sure of that." McClary nodded.

John Stark turned to face the men standing around the powder cart. "I thank ye for your good services. When we've unloaded the powder, you can have your cart and oxen and return home—if you desire."

Demeritt cleared his throat. "I think I speak for my friends, Colonel. If you'll have us, we'd be mightily pleased to lend a hand here today."

"And we would be mightily pleased to have ye," Stark replied emphatically. "Reed's regiment at Charlestown

Neck is under strength. You'd be of great use there. Reed's ailing, and officers are needed. In fact, you're all needed."

"Any place. Any place," Ira eagerly cut in. "I'll help, if I can. You name it. I'll be there."

A corporal was directed to guide the men to Reed's regiment. Caleb, his father said, would be kept here for the present, until it was decided what to do with him.

Although Caleb regretted being parted from his friends, he also was pleased to be retained in his father's regiment. It was only a temporary arrangement, Caleb realized, and he might be sent packing at any moment. But in the meantime, here he was in the thick of things. If events kept moving at their present pace, Caleb hoped that his father would be far too busy to worry about him.

As John Stark and McClary stood with Caleb, a dispatch rider came galloping up with a message for the Colonel. After reading it carefully, Stark placed the dispatch in an inside pocket. "Tell General Ward I'll have my men on the march within the hour," he directed the rider, who immediately wheeled his horse about and headed back toward Cambridge. "The British are making ready to embark from Boston," Stark said tersely. "They'll no doubt try to take Breed's Hill. Two hundred of my regiment are needed as reinforcements."

McClary frowned. "Only two hundred?"

"I have a feeling this is only the beginning," Stark replied. "Before this day's done, every man jack of us will be committed. But for now, it's only two hundred." He turned to one of the sentries. "Request Lieutenant Colonel Wyman to report here at once."

"Wyman's a good man," McClary said. "You'll put him in command of this first group?"

Stark nodded. "And in the meantime I want every company put on the alert. We must be ready to move out at a moment's notice. Will you see to that, Andrew—and also pass the word to Reed's regiment?"

"Rely on me, John," McClary said quietly. He put his hand on Caleb's shoulder. "What's to be done with the lad here?"

Stark's voice was impatient. "Do? Do as ye will. Every one of us must be put to good use." He glared at Caleb. "Take care of yourself, ye hear?"

Caleb drew himself erect. "Yes, sir."

"See to him, Andrew," Stark growled. He did an abrupt about-face and hurried up the steps to his headquarters.

Alone with Caleb, McClary grinned at him. "I was hoping he'd leave your assignment to my discretion. Captain Moore's company is understrength and that's no doubt where you'll eventually be assigned. But for now I'm putting you in Captain Henry Dearborn's company. You know him?"

Caleb thought for a moment. "Is he that young doctor from Nottingham? I've heard good reports of him."

"He's a fine officer," McClary assured him. "There's a corporal in his company who's an old friend of yours."

Caleb puzzled over the identity of this mysterious corporal as he shouldered his musket and walked with Mc-Clary toward a large old house, once occupied by a Tory family and now used by Captain Dearborn's company. Just before mounting the steps, Caleb was startled by a high-pitched whoop, followed by a rasping voice calling his name. No mistaking that voice!

"Eli!" Caleb exclaimed, as the squat, bald-headed companion of the Portsmouth adventure flung his arms about Caleb and pounded his back.

"By jinks, boy," Eli exclaimed, "how do ye always manage to turn up jest in time for action?"

"You do have a nose for trouble, Caleb," McClary said. He spoke gravely to Eli. "There's big doings afoot. The Colonel thinks we'll all be fighting beyond Charlestown Neck before the day's done. Redcoats are being ferried out now. I'm going to tell Captain Dearborn the news. Meantime, you'd best prepare your squad for action."

Eli jerked a thumb toward Caleb. "What about him?"

"Unless Captain Dearborn tells you no, I'd say Caleb's now a member of your squad—even though we don't have time to swear him in proper." McClary saluted Caleb casually. "Good luck."

Caleb drew himself to attention and returned the salute smartly.

"By jolley," Eli said, as McClary walked up the stairs leading to Dearborn's headquarters, "you make a better-looking soldier than the Major does."

Caleb smiled. "I suppose what counts is how a man looks in action."

"The Major looks real good then," Eli admitted. He turned quickly away. "Well, I better go tell the men to get ready—though how ready we'll be, I jest don't know."

"You're having trouble?" Caleb asked.

"Trouble? I guess we're having trouble! Every man in the squad's got a different style musket. There's the Brown Bess, some old snaphances, wheel locks, a fusee. And the standard ball they give us jest won't do. We have to hammer each ball to fit our own musket size. And as for gunpowder, that's getting to be as rare as pearls."

"But I just helped bring in a load of powder," Caleb said quickly. "We brought in twenty barrels from Madbury. It's the powder we took from the fort!"

Eli beamed. "Ye don't say! By jinks, that's the best news I've heard since the old cow ate Bessie's bonnet. Mebbe now we can git down to some serious fighting!"

17

At 1 P.M. an express rider arrived with the order that Colonel Stark had been expecting. His entire regiment was to proceed at once to the Charlestown peninsula, to help oppose a steadily growing British force that was being landed at Morton's Point.

Caleb marched beside Eli in Captain Dearborn's company, which was first in the line of march. A few ranks ahead of him, leading the regiment, he could see his father walking with Major McClary and Captain Dearborn. Marching directly ahead of Caleb was young Goffe Moore, the drummer boy. The *rat-a-tat-tat* of his drum merged with a booming cannonade that increased in volume as this sweltering hot day wore on.

The roar of cannon became louder as they marched along the dusty road and started the long descent to Charlestown Neck. Soon it appeared that the drummer boy was playing his quick step in pantomime. Caleb saw men's lips move, but he heard no sound come from them. They were marching deeper into a vortex of crashing, thundering sound that pressed like a physical force on Caleb's eardrums. Ahead of them, a cannon ball ripped into a tree, shattering its top, and bounced into a field. As Caleb involuntarily flinched, Eli shouted in his ear, "Don't fret about the balls that miss ye. Ye'll have no time for that."

"Nor about the one that hits me," Caleb shouted back. "I'll surely have no time for that."

Eli whacked him on the back. "You're the one, lad," he shouted. "Always ready with a jest."

Caleb managed a wry smile. Truth to tell, he was terribly frightened. But if a smile could mask his fear, he'd get by.

As the downward grade leveled out onto a broad plain, their marching column passed the juncture of a road leading to Cambridge. Here several knots of armed men, evidently under no central direction, joined them. The tree-lined road was becoming crowded. Their pace slowed, as they marched toward a tangle of troops clustered tight together near a spot where the line of trees ended and the road dipped toward the narrow Neck—now being raked by sustained fire from British ships. It was evident that the troops blocking the way had no intention of venturing out onto that exposed strip of land. Soon Stark's regiment was brought to a complete halt.

Eli grasped Caleb by the arm and pulled him forward through the press until they had reached John Stark's side. The Colonel was livid with rage. "Move!" he shouted to the crowded men. "You're blocking our way!" They regarded him with dull interest. His voice didn't carry over the cannons' roar, and in any event this angry man in homespun was no leader that these Massachusetts troops felt obliged to recognize.

"It's no use," McClary shouted to Stark. "They won't budge."

"By gorry, I'll budge 'em!" Stark shouted back. "Captain Dearborn! Get your company on the move! We'll march through this rabble, or over 'em! It makes small difference to me."

All up and down the line, sergeants and corporals were given the word. "March! Forward march!" And march they did—grim, resolute troops plunging forward into the disorganized mass that blocked their way. The roadblock abruptly dissolved, as the men scattered to the sides of the road.

The New Hampshiremen marched straight down to the Neck with Stark, McClary, and Dearborn leading the way. Eli and Caleb were not far behind, marching abreast of the drummer boy, who beat a spirited though seemingly noiseless tattoo. Icy shivers raced along Caleb's spine as they moved into the open space beyond the trees. Here he obtained his first full view of the long, narrow neck of land they had to cross. It was barely thirty yards wide, with neither trees nor shrubs for cover. The thin road traversing its center was pitted and cratered. Dirt leaped from the road as cannon balls ripped into its surface. Muddy geysers spurted from marshy land at both sides where some balls missed their marks. The waters of the Mystic River on the left of the neck and of a millpond on the right were in a state of continuous agitation, as misdirected balls fell into their depths. Looking beyond a rock and pile causeway that formed the tide milldam, Caleb saw that much of this solid shot was coming from a wide cove leading to the Charles River. Two gundalows, which the British had converted into floating batteries by mounting four 24-pounders on each boat, had been rowed up to the causeway and were spitting smoke and flame. From the cove's center, the eighteen-gun warship *Symmetry* blasted the Neck at short range. Farther out in the Charles River, the battleship *Glasgow*, with its tiers of cannon, directed thunderous, long-range salvos at the thin strip of land.

It seemed impossible that any troops could cross that beleaguered ground without suffering a major loss. But Caleb saw that his father, McClary and Dearborn were walking toward it side by side at a steady pace. Caleb involuntarily slowed his step and glanced at Eli beside him. He was surprised to see a wide, toothless grin on his friend's face.

"You enjoying yourself?" Caleb shouted.

Eli put his mouth close to Caleb's ear. "I'm that scairt,

I'm most sick," he admitted. "But we're in the front rank and must set the pace. Come ahead, lad. Don't falter."

Caleb adjusted his step to Eli's. He even managed to form a half-hearted grin, as he saw the drummer boy turn his pale face toward him. The boy smiled weakly in return and beat his drum fiercely.

Now they were at the Neck. The marshy ground quivered beneath their feet like a living thing, as shot thudded along its length. Cannon ball screamed overhead. Chain shot and ring shot whined about them. They were engulfed in sound. Caleb felt like a figure in a nightmare. All his senses told him to run. Run away from this place. Run for his very life. But he could not run. He must follow the slow—agonizingly slow—pace of the leaders. Wasn't his pa human? Couldn't he see the need for speed?

A cannon ball crashed into a boulder a rod away, skittered across the road, and splashed into the Mystic. Caleb involuntarily quickened his pace. He was now almost abreast of Captain Dearborn, so close that he could hear the Captain as he shouted at John Stark, "Suggest we move at double quick."

Those were Caleb's exact sentiments. He looked hopefully toward his father, but John Stark shook his head. "I'll not tire my men," he replied. "One fresh man's worth ten fatigued ones." And he kept his steady pace. Just like he's out for a Sunday stroll, Caleb thought. He certainly was learning the strength of his father's character this day. He hoped the lesson would not prove fatal.

Finally, unbelievably, they were nearing the end of Charlestown Neck. A few more steps and they were on the peninsula, walking along a broad dirt road that was bordered by fields of high grass.

Caleb turned to Eli. "We made it!"

"Aye." Eli's voice was a harsh croak. "We made it—thus far."

As Caleb turned to survey the inferno through which

they had just passed, Eli swung him about roughly. "Look ahead," he urged, "never backward."

Caleb nodded dumbly. He could see the reason for that. The brief glimpse he had just been permitted was a shocking one. He had seen the slowly moving line of troops hesitate mometarily, as one man leaped into the air, his mouth open wide in a soundless scream, and then tumble headfirst into the muck.

Caleb attempted to erase the picture from his mind. He would concentrate on what lay ahead. This day must be lived minute by minute. Ahead of them, the road swung to the right, passing between scattered dwellings, on its way to the distant village of Charlestown. A narrow carriage track, forking off to the left of this main road, ascended Bunker Hill. It was this path that Stark, McClary, and Dearborn elected to take. The troops followed, passing through waist-high pasture grass on each side of the road. It was a hot climb. The sweat ran down Caleb's back. His jacket clung to him. Looking toward Eli at his right, he saw that his friend's face was flushed and that a bead of perspiration quivered on the end of his nose.

Eli mopped his face with a swipe of his jacket sleeve. "Could have picked a cooler day to fight," he grumbled.

Caleb noticed that, although it still was necessary to talk loudly, the overpowering roar of battle they had experienced on Charlestown Neck diminished as they mounted Bunker Hill.

"We promised the lobsterbacks a warm reception," Caleb said.

Eli grunted in reply. He was concentrating his full attention on climbing the hill.

Finally they stood on the broad, grassy hilltop, in company with a large number of men. Caleb estimated that there must be over a thousand of them—some at work building breastworks but many standing on the brow of the hill, staring toward the east. As Stark, with his two officers, were among this latter group, Eli and Caleb climbed a few remaining yards to stand beside them.

A panoramic view spread out below them. Halfway across the peninsula, to their right, was a smaller hill that Eli identified as Breed's Hill. Here the Americans had built their redoubt, a long sturdy fortress with earthen walls. It was the target for a continuous rain of solid shot from the four British ships of the line that lay anchored in the river. Cannon situated on Copp's Hill in Boston, across the Charles River, also were firing on the fort. Glancing in that direction, it seemed to Caleb that most of Boston's population must be gathered to gawk at the pending battle. The rooftops of houses along the Boston shore line were swarming with spectators.

Looking down the eastern slope of Bunker Hill, Caleb saw a marshy spot at its bottom and, beyond that, a tree-lined, grassy field. In the middle of this field, some men were strengthening a rail fence that extended from the cart track to the south of Bunker Hill, went straight across the field, and ended at a bluff overlooking a narrow beach along the Mystic River.

Caleb's throat contracted as he looked beyond the fence, toward a bare rise of ground at the far tip of the peninsula. On the crest of this rise, which Eli called Morton's Hill, Caleb for the first time saw British troops drawn up in full battle array. Row on row they stood—toy soldiers at this distance, with their bayonets, red coats, and white gaiters bright in the afternoon sun. Beyond the nub of land on which they stood, Caleb watched three large rowboats, crowded with redcoated soldiers, prepare to land at Morton's Point. Other boats, that had already discharged their troops, were being rowed back toward the Boston docks, to pick up waiting reinforcements. Cannon balls arched above these troop carriers, as the British ships fired toward the Americans dug in on Breed's Hill.

John Stark pointed toward the rail fence at the bottom of

Bunker Hill. "Look at that," he said in a disgusted voice. "There's the natural path for General Howe's troops to take from Morton's Point—if they plan to flank us. That fence looks to be practically unmanned for a hundred and fifty yards nearest the river. What sort of defense is that? If there are over two hundred men down there, I'll eat my hat. There must be depth—at least a three-man depth—all along that fence."

"You're right, John," McClary agreed. "How many men shall we commit to the rail fence?"

"Every last one of us," Stark growled. "Pass the word."

Stark's regiment walked down the hill, through waist-high grass, in straggling disorder. The lack of formation didn't bother Stark, who was intent only on reaching the rail fence as quickly as possible. Eli and Caleb were close behind him as the Colonel strode up to a kneeling soldier who was busily stuffing hay between the upper and lower fence rails. The soldier paused in his work and looked up sourly at John Stark.

"Took ye long enough to git here," the soldier observed. He shifted his wad of tobacco and spat against the fence. "Captain Knowlton wanted reinforcements long before this."

Caleb felt a growing anger. He expected no huzzas for coming to the side of these men, some of whom must have been toiling here all day, but he did expect to be received with some show of courtesy. John Stark, however, did not seem affronted by his reception. "Captain Knowlton, you say? Then you must be from General Putnam's Connecticut troops."

Slowly the lanky soldier rose to his feet. "We are. And who the devil are you?"

"Colonel Stark," Caleb heard his father say in a level tone, "of the First New Hampshires."

The soldier looked startled, and then grinned broadly as he reached forward and pumped Stark's hand. "John

Stark!" he exclaimed. "The tales I've heard of you! I'm that proud to shake your hand. I'm Clem Dawson."

"Glad to meet you," Stark replied agreeably. While he talked to the soldier, his eyes ranged up and down the rail fence, where many of his New Hampshiremen were already at work. A quantity of hay had been cut and left in the field by Charlestown farmers who had neither time nor inclination to complete their haying. Some of the men were stuffing this between the top and bottom fence rails, together with clods of dirt and brush. The soldiers' frontier instincts governed their actions, as they tried to make this fence appear a good deal more solid than it was. They needed no direct orders to accomplish this. Indeed, when young Captain Knowlton came rushing up, attempting to direct their activity, not a man left his post. The Captain was referred to Colonel Stark, standing on the rise above them.

Stark, watching this byplay, was agreeably surprised when Knowlton approached and introduced himself in a friendly manner. He shook the young man's hand.

"I didn't intend to overstep my bounds, Colonel," Knowlton said. "I realize these men are under your command. But since General Putnam has sent you here as my reinforcements—"

"Stop right there," Stark quickly interrupted. "Old Put had naught to do with your reinforcements. This was strictly my own notion. I saw that you hold an important position, and since you're undermanned we've come to help."

The captain looked uncomfortable but managed to reply in a steady voice. "I thank you, sir. But the fact remains, I am in command here."

"Command your Connecticut men, and good luck to ye," Stark said crisply. "Just see they don't get in the way of my troops."

"I grant that you are my senior in command," Knowlton said stiffly, "but it's also true that General Putnam is your senior."

Stark rapidly was losing patience. "Blast it, man, I don't care who's senior in command. There's a battle to be won, and we're wasting time." He glared at Knowlton. "I suggest you get back to your own troops."

Knowlton's smile was bitter. "I seem to have small choice."

McClary stepped forward. "Things will work out, Captain. We're with ye all the way. As Gentleman Johnny Burgoyne says, just give us elbow room."

As Knowlton's face reddened with suppressed anger, McClary winked at him and hurried after Stark and Dearborn, who already were striding down the hill toward the rail fence.

Eli nudged Caleb. "Come on. We'll miss out on the action."

"Small chance of that," Caleb grumbled, following Eli down the hill, a few steps behind McClary.

They occupied themselves for the next few minutes in gathering armloads of sweet-smelling hay from the field and stuffing it between the rails. The sun beat down and the hay itched where it came in contact with Caleb's sweaty skin. He yearned for a drink of cool, fresh water. A high grassy bank sloped steeply toward the Mystic River, and Caleb wondered if he dared drink the river water. As he considered this, he was startled to see his father climb up the bank from the beach below. Had he been thirsty too?

The next moment he realized that his father was concerned with far greater matters than a dry throat. "There's no defense on the beach!" Stark shouted to Major McClary. "We must have a breastwork built there, straight across the beach."

Before McClary had a chance to relay Stark's order, the

New Hampshiremen within earshot were already dragging stones from a long stone wall behind them and carrying them toward the bank. During the next half hour, Caleb and Eli worked steadily in a seemingly endless procession of men, carrying stones from the wall, over the eight-foot bank, to the beach. It was hot, hard work. Caleb's arms ached and he had difficulty straightening his fingers after he had relinquished a stone. But there was an urgency about this task that tapped hidden reserves of strength.

Finally it was done—a stone breastwork stretching across a narrow beach that, although barely twelve feet wide at high tide, would furnish ample room for a British light-infantry column. John Stark regarded the stonework with satisfaction. "It should give us a fighting chance." He glanced toward the dark waters of the Mystic River at his left and at the high bank on his right. "We're the cork in the bottle at this point," he said. "If I were in Howe's place, I'd be throwing some of my best troops against this spot." He looked around him at his troops strung out along the beach. "I'll take personal command here. I want only volunteers to stay with me."

Not a man moved from his place. They all have faith in my pa, Caleb thought proudly.

"I don't hanker to be no stopper in a bottle," Eli whispered in his ear, "but I'm jest too tired to climb that blessed bank again."

18

John Stark leaped over the stone wall, walked forward forty paces, and hammered a stake into the sand. "Here's the limit," he declared. "Don't fire till the first regular reaches that stake."

Returning to his troops, he formed his best marksmen in three ranks behind the stone wall, each rank stretching from beach to bank. The rest were put in reserve, a short distance to the rear. Caleb, assigned to this latter group, enviously watched Eli in the second rank as Stark issued instructions. When the enemy approached, the first rank was to kneel, the second to stoop, and the third to remain standing. Caleb knew from earlier talks with his father that this was a tested method to ensure continuous firing, used by Rogers' Rangers during the French and Indian War. The plan was for the first rank to fire, then the second, and finally the third. Due to the position of the marksmen, each row would fire over the men ahead. As the last rank discharged its muskets, the men in the first row would have had time to reload. The British army didn't bother with such complicated firing tactics. Its regulars relied primarily on the bayonet and paid little attention to taking true aim when firing their muskets.

As the Colonel was completing his instructions, Caleb's attention was distracted by heavy black smoke rising in the distance. The high bank cut off his view, but the smoke seemed to be coming from the far southeastern end of the peninsula.

"Charlestown's afire!" a young soldier shouted down to them from the top of the bank.

"Stand your ground!" Stark ordered, as several of his men on the beach started toward the bank. "I want Major McClary," he shouted to the young soldier.

A few moments later McClary scrambled down to the sand and reported to John Stark. The entire village was ablaze, he said. British ships were lobbing red-hot cannon balls into Charlestown, and the battery on Copp's Hill in Boston was using balls filled with burning pitch, called carcasses, to bombard the town.

It seemed to Caleb an inhuman way to clear the town of snipers. Indeed, the closer he came to actual battle, the less glamorous it seemed. War, he was beginning to realize, was a hard, brutal business, with destruction as its goal. No amount of individual bravery could mask its ugly face. Resolutely, Caleb put these thoughts from his mind. This was no way for a soldier to think before going into battle. He must learn to hate. He must become so filled with rage that he would not hesitate to kill. He was surprised to feel a sudden trembling in his legs. I'm afraid, he told himself. No matter how hard I try to hate, deep down I'm afraid. Surprisingly, he felt less tense after making this admission. He wondered if his father's legs had ever trembled before a battle.

Captain Dearborn looked over the bank. "They're starting to move up, Colonel! Shall I post an observer for you?"

"Thank you, Henry," Stark called back, "but I'll serve as my own observer." He turned to his men. "Stay in position," he ordered. "I'll keep ye informed." The next moment he was scrambling up the bank.

He was visible to the men on the beach, as he stood above them, looking eastward toward Morton's Hill. "They're on their way, lads," he called down. "About a half mile off. Row on row of 'em, with bayonets fixed. They find it hard to hold their ranks. There's fences to climb, and they look to be wearing full field equipment. I think Howe himself is at their head! Behind him march the light infantry. There must be over three hundred. Howe's own Welsh Fusiliers lead the way! Behind them are the grenadiers. No mistaking their black bearskin hats. Next, there's two regiments of regulars. It's an attack in force. No question."

John Stark remained on the bank, describing the British advance, until the troops reached a spot a quarter of a mile away. He gave a sharp exclamation, then, and jumped down to the sand. "The light infantry's filing off onto the beach! Get ready for action!"

As the three ranks of men behind the stone barricade assumed their firing positions, Caleb looked anxiously up the narrow strip of beach. Now he had his first close-up view of the enemy, a flying column of light infantry charging forward at frightening speed. Caleb recalled that these men were reputed to be among the best troops in the British army. The beach was swarming with them—redcoats beneath a gleaming forest of bayonets. The flying column formed into quick-stepping ranks, fifteen men across. The men on the far right splashed through the shallow waters of the Mystic.

As they approached the stake that Stark had driven into the beach, the British soldiers leveled their bayonets. Caleb's finger itched to pull the trigger of his musket. Now they were past the stake, so close that Caleb could make out individual features.

"Fire!" John Stark roared the command.

The New Hampshiremen crouched behind the wall fired a volley as they had been trained to do—first, second, third rank in order—firing so quickly that a solid sheet of smoke and flame seemed to erupt above the wall. The concentrated fire devastated the first rank of charging light infantry. The soldiers fell backward as if punched by a giant fist.

Caleb found a place for himself in the third rank, squeezed in next to the bank. His musket fire now formed part of the solid blast of flame that was decimating the light infantry, as rank after rank marched stoically forward over the bodies of their dead and wounded. Groans and screams mingled with the steady crack of the American muskets.

Why don't they return our fire? Caleb wondered. He learned later that Howe had ordered a bayonet charge. Never before had opposing troops been able to reload fast enough to prevent successive waves of British troops from pressing forward with cold steel. Caleb was witnessing a hard new lesson in warfare. But at this crucial moment, he was far too busy to ponder its meaning.

The cream of Howe's forces continued to advance on the stone wall—and all met the same fate. Bodies were piling one on top of one another in the sand before the stone barricade.

For Caleb, time stood still in this purgatory to which he was assigned. Load and reload the smoking hot musket. Fire and fire again into the advancing ranks. Would they never stop coming?

The British now were firing back in desultory fashion. Several balls whistled past Caleb's head. Suddenly the man standing next to him in the smoke-shrouded line of marksmen screamed in pain and dropped to the ground, clutching his shoulder. As Caleb knelt to assist him, he heard a shout from farther down the line. "Colonel Stark! Your boy's been hit!"

Before Caleb could make a denial, he heard his father's stern voice. "Keep firing! Heed only the enemy!"

"I'm all right, Pa!" Caleb cried, but his voice was drowned in a blast of musket fire.

Eventually it was over. These well-trained British troops were, after all, only flesh and blood. Though their officers cursed them and hit them with the flat of their swords, there came a time when human will could no longer carry them forward to certain execution. Retreat was ordered. The British soldiers staggered back down the beach, carrying their wounded.

Behind the stone wall, the hot, powder-grimed New Hampshiremen sank down upon the sand. As Caleb wearily knelt beside the wounded soldier, attempting to stanch the blood flowing from a ragged gash in the man's shoulder, he heard his name being called. Looking up, he saw his father walking across the beach, looking intently at individual faces.

"Here, sir!" Caleb called.

As he heard Caleb's voice, a rare smile creased John Stark's face. In a moment, he was kneeling beside his son, both hands gripping Caleb's arms, as if to assure himself that his boy truly was sound and whole.

"I'm all right," Caleb said.

"I'm that glad," his father softly replied. "I can't tell ye how glad." Abruptly he turned to the wounded soldier beside Caleb. "But there's some not so well off."

"I'll survive," the soldier said weakly.

"Of course ye will, but we must get ye back to Cambridge for proper care." Briskly the Colonel summoned two of his company to carry off the wounded man. "Our losses are light, praise be," he said to Caleb. Looking beyond the stone barricade at the enemy dead, sprawled two deep in places, his face became grim. "Howe can't say the same. Never have I seen sheep lie as thick in the fold."

They both looked up at the bank as McClary's booming voice called down to them. " 'Twas a grand defense!"

"Aye. Ye might call it so," Stark called back. "They'll not be eager to rush this pile of rock again. How do you fare, behind the fence?"

"I'll know shortly," McClary reported. "They're advancing on us, but they're still all of two hundred yards off. They held up, waiting for their light infantry to flank us along the beach—but you spoiled that."

Stark looked about him. "You'll need our help. I'll leave a token force here at the rocks."

"No, John," McClary protested. "Your men are done in."

"We'll take our rest behind your fence," Stark assured him. His voice sharpened, as he ordered his men up the bank. With groans and muttered curses, his exhausted troops obeyed. Caleb, assisted by Eli's helping hand, was among the first to clamber up the bluff. Tired as he was, he had no wish to be part of the token force at the wall, with only the dead for company. He could not long endure the fearful reproach in those wide-open, staring eyes.

Caleb was amazed at the number of troops that had gathered behind the long rail fence. He learned later that almost fifteen hundred men were here. They appeared to greatly outnumber the slowly approaching British, who were fanned out in a double line with the grenadiers leading the way. Again, as at the stone wall, the redcoats were making slow headway over the walls and fences that crisscrossed the fields.

Major McClary, who had stationed himself behind the section of fence where Caleb now knelt next to Eli, urged his New Hampshiremen to hold their fire.

Farther down the line, behind the Connecticut troops, Caleb could see a portly, square-jawed officer astride a white horse, shouting orders to his men. As he was the only mounted man behind their lines, he presented a tempting target, but he seemed oblivious to danger. Spurring his horse back and forth behind the fence, he at one point approached near enough for Caleb to hear his shouted command. "Don't fire till you see the whites of their eyes!"

Caleb nudged Eli. "Who's that officer?"

Eli looked astonished. "Ye don't know? That's General Israel Putnam, in person. Old Put. You'd best remember him."

As the British leveled their bayonets and approached within musket range, Caleb felt his trigger finger tense, just as it had at the stone wall. He resisted the impulse, but farther down the fence he heard one musket discharge and then another. Old Put screamed his displeasure, and behind Caleb the stern voice of McClary urged his men to wait for his orders.

Now the redcoats, approaching at quick pace through

the waist-high grass, were so close that Caleb felt sure he could indeed see the whites of their eyes. They were near enough for Caleb to hear a British officer, in clipped English accent, shout to his men, "Hold your fire! We'll take them with bare steel!"

The next instant, Caleb heard old Put's barked order. "Fire!" The order immediately was echoed by officers up and down the line, and once again Caleb saw the results of Yankee marksmanship. A solid blast of musket fire along the entire length of the fence mowed down the first rank of British troops like hay before the scythe. The moans of the wounded assaulted his ears. His fingers trembled and cold sweat ran in rivulets down his back as he reloaded his musket. Through a swirling white curtain of musket smoke, he could see the second rank of grenadiers moving steadily forward. All about him men were firing and reloading quickly, with no attempt to maintain the steady firing discipline that he had seen at the stone wall. Yet there were so many troops concentrated behind the fence that this individual firing produced an impenetrable defense. British troops reeled and broke. Most of the regulars in the second rank now were sprawled in agony among their comrades in the blood-soaked hayfield.

Events of this day remained mixed in Caleb's mind. The fighting seemed to last for an interminable period, although he learned later that the battle was concluded before six that afternoon. He knew that they threw back two attacks in force at the rail fence and that, after a deadly period of waiting, light infantry paused a respectful distance from the fence and fired upon them. This, as it turned out, was diversionary fire, for the bulk of the advancing British troops —reinforced now by fresh reserves from Boston—wheeled left before reaching the fence. They launched an assault on the Breed's Hill breastwork and redoubt, where a small company under the command of Colonel William Prescott had been throwing back repeated attacks.

Now there was only scattered fire coming from the rail fence. John Stark was pacing back and forth behind his men, urging them not to fire an unnecessary shot. They were desperately short of ammunition. Caleb had only two musket balls left and just enough powder to fire them. All about him, men were in the same predicament. Eli's powder was completely exhausted.

His father paused for a moment behind Caleb. "Win or lose, we've made a proud showing here today. I want to thank ye for bringing the powder. Without it, our muskets would long since have been silent."

Caleb's weary face broke into a grin. "I'm most grateful myself for that powder. I wish we could have brought double the load."

"Aye," Stark agreed, "with ample powder, we'd truly show 'em what fighters we cowardly farmers can be." He looked sharply toward Breed's Hill, as several men came running from the redoubt, pursued by British soldiers, and raced down the hill toward the far end of the rail fence. "The devils are in the redoubt!" he exclaimed. "Our boys up there must be clean out of powder." He raised his voice. "Look sharp, men! Prescott's troops are on the run! Use your last grain of powder to cover them!"

Once again Caleb was plunged into the midst of battle. As the defenders of Breed's Hill ran past the rail fence, on their way to the comparative safety of Bunker Hill, Caleb fired his last two bullets at pursuing redcoats. The British soldiers hesitated momentarily, as troops all along the fence opened spasmodic fire. In this one afternoon, the British had acquired a deep respect for Yankee muskets. Although the brief diversion helped Prescott's troops to outdistance their pursuers, it left the men behind the rail fence in jeopardy.

"Back! Fall back!" Stark ordered. "To the Neck!"

As Eli and Caleb ran together toward the cart track at

the base of Bunker Hill, Caleb glanced quickly toward his father. While his men were obeying the order to retreat, John Stark had banded together with McClary and Dearborn. With the last of their ammunition, these three officers were firing toward the approaching British. Their fire, although pitifully inadequate to cover a retreat, nonetheless did momentarily slow the redcoats.

Caleb heard musket balls whistle all about him as he raced along the narrow cart track. Grapeshot from British artillery whined through the air. Fearful that this retreat was turning into a rout, Caleb was heartened to see a sizable number of American troops rushing toward them, down the slope of Bunker Hill. Judging from their fresh appearance and the prodigal use they were making of their muskets, it was apparent that these were reserve troops. The full ammunition pouches of these soldiers saved the day for the retreating defenders of the rail fence, as the British hesitated once more when faced with accurate musket fire.

Although Charlestown Neck still was under heavy bombardment, Caleb and Eli raced across its cratered surface with scant thought for incoming cannon balls. Caleb had the feeling that once they reached its opposite end they would be home safe.

His feeling proved to be correct, for the British had suffered terrible losses on Charlestown peninsula. They had no desire at that moment to test the rebel defenses around Cambridge.

Eli and Caleb paused by the side of Medford road as it began its long ascent to Ploughed Hill and looked down anxiously on a long line of soldiers straggling off the peninsula. It was a pitiful column, bloodied and weary.

Suddenly Eli pointed a stubby finger. "By chowder! I see 'em!"

Looking in the direction of Eli's pointing finger, Caleb

gave a whoop. "They're safe!" Walking side by side, he saw his father, McClary, and Dearborn approach the bottom of the hill. Unbelievably, they seemed unharmed. "Pa!" Caleb called. His voice was lost in the incessant cannonade from British ships, but John Stark noticed Caleb's frantically waving hand.

As the three officers approached with measured stride, Caleb thought that never before had he seen his father's face so gray and weary. Captain Dearborn too seemed drained of vitality. Only McClary appeared to be his usual robust self. He roared a greeting to Eli and Caleb and put a hamlike hand on each of their shoulders.

The Colonel looked at his son through sunken, dark-rimmed eyes that still retained an icy glint. "You fought well," he said quietly. "You're a true Stark."

Caleb fought back sudden tears. He remained silent, unwilling to risk a reply.

McClary, looking off toward the peninsula, frowned as he observed activity on Bunker Hill. "What are the lobster-backs up to now?" he growled. "Are they making ready to come at us?"

"I don't think so, Andrew," Dearborn answered in a weary voice. "Let's get back to camp."

"In a moment. I'd like a closer look at 'em. Down at the old pound, this side of the Neck, there's a fine vantage point."

Stark sounded exasperated. "Your fine vantage point is also a fine place to be hit. It's within range of the ships."

"The ball's not yet cast that will kill me," McClary assured him. "I'll be only a moment. Will ye wait?"

"Not I," Stark replied shortly. "I hear we're putting up breastworks at Winter Hill. I'll be needed there." He turned to Dearborn. "Why don't you, and Caleb and Eli, stay with our anxious friend."

McClary grinned and started off at a fast pace down the

road. "I'll be back before ye miss me," he shouted back at them.

The three who remained at the roadside watched Stark as he began his long uphill climb on the Medford road. Then they turned their attention toward the entrance to Charlestown Neck. Soon they could see McClary climb onto a high fence at the old pound. The Major, atop his fence, gazed off toward Bunker Hill for what seemed to be an interminably long time.

"He's a perfect target," Dearborn growled. "Why won't he climb down?"

When McClary finally did jump back to the ground, Caleb gave a sigh of relief. The Major's luck had held. Now perhaps they all could go back to camp. He hoped there would be victuals prepared. And plenty of water. He was that thirsty, he could drink a well dry.

Then it happened. A random cannon ball, shot from the battleship *Glasgow*, hit a buttonwood tree a short distance from McClary. Caleb saw the heavy ball glance off the tree and strike the Major with terrible force. It passed directly through his abdomen and skittered across the ground behind him. McClary threw up his hands, jumped high in the air, and fell forward on his face. The ball must have killed him instantly.

Captain Dearborn already was running down the hill, toward the Major's body. Caleb and Eli raced alongside him.

"Why?" Caleb cried as he ran. "Oh, God! Why?"

Caleb sat at a long table in his father's headquarters, quill pen poised over a sheet of paper, as John Stark pondered his next words. It was the morning of June 19, two days after the battle. Feverish activity at Winter Hill was subsiding, as it became apparent that the British were not preparing an immediate attack on the American forces.

Caleb had been sure, when he had first received the summons to visit his father, that this meant the end of his stay at Winter Hill. Instead, to his immense relief, he had found that his father merely wished to utilize the writing ability that Caleb had acquired from Reverend Pickels.

Now Caleb sat with pen in hand, as he had for the better part of an hour, while his father slowly dictated a letter concerning the battle to the Honorable Matthew Thornton, President of the New Hampshire Provincial Congress. Words did not come easily to John Stark. He considered each sentence until he was sure that his meaning was clear. It was evident that the letter's conclusion was a difficult one. Caleb fidgeted as his father gazed into space, weighing the words he would trust to paper. To Caleb's surprise, the words finally came in a rush, as if his father wanted this part of the message over and done with. Caleb's pen scratched frantically on the paper.

"A number of officers and men of my regiment were killed and wounded," he wrote. "The officers killed were Major McClary, by a cannon ball; Captain Baldwin and Lieutenant Scott by small arms. The whole number killed and missing—fifteen. Wounded—forty five. Total—sixty."

Again there was a pause. "We remain in good spirits. Where we have lost one, the enemy has lost three." Colonel Stark sighed and visibly relaxed in his chair. "That's it. Does it state the facts plain and true?"

"I believe so," Caleb replied. He hesitated. "Except that I can't say I remain in good spirits."

"Nor I," his father agreed. "I should say that our resolve remains high." He looked soberly at Caleb. "It's been a punishing blow, losing two good friends in one afternoon. Fred Baldwin and Andrew McClary were both old comrades."

"And was it worthwhile?" The words were out of Caleb's mouth before he had time to reflect. But he did not regret this question, which had been in his mind ever since the terrible slaughter at the stone wall.

John Stark did not appear annoyed. He thought carefully before answering, slowly rubbing his chin. In the quiet room, Caleb could hear the rasp of his father's fingers on gray stubble. Flies buzzed, and a hornet bumped angrily against the windowpane. When Stark finally broke the silence, he spoke softly, as if talking to himself. Caleb leaned forward to catch his words. "Was it worthwhile? We proved that we could meet 'em on their own terms and beat 'em. We did that at the stone wall and rail fence. It was diamond scratch diamond all the way. I'd say that was worthwhile. We gained a new spirit; they gained a new caution. And that was worthwhile. We died, and they died, and the worms profited. Is that worthwhile?" Stark sighed. "I'm growing older, and with each passing year the doubt grows." Slowly he raised his head and gazed fiercely at Caleb. His voice strengthened. "But I do know there must be values. Without values, life is useless. We might as well be dead. And if a man gives his life to assure these values for other men, who's to say that's not worthwhile?"

Caleb stared wide-eyed at his father, momentarily speechless.

John Stark rose from his chair. With an obvious effort, he concentrated his attention on the paper that Caleb held in his hand. "Let's make a finished copy of that letter," he said.

Caleb also rose. "Yes sir."

"And, Caleb—" Once again Stark's brisk manner seemed to desert him. His look was beseeching. "Don't ye think you should be getting back to Gramp's house?"

Caleb lowered his gaze. He'd been expecting this, and he knew the futility of further argument. "If you think I should," he said in a low voice.

"It's not that I don't want ye here," Stark said quickly. "But the old man—" He glanced toward the door, as a loud knock drew his attention. "Come in," he called.

The soldier who entered saluted in a half-hearted manner. "Man by the name of Captain Page says he wants to see you, sir."

Caleb's mouth popped open. "Speak of the devil!"

"Send him in," Stark directed. He winked at Caleb as the soldier departed. "I'll not tell Gramp what ye just called him."

A moment later Captain Page entered, dust-covered and puffing. He started toward his son-in-law and then blinked as he saw Caleb. "Bless my buttons!" he exclaimed. "Caleb!" With two strides he was next to the boy and pressing him close to his dusty greatcoat. "You're safe and well!"

Caleb sneezed but did not pull away. He could scarcely believe this greeting. His grandfather then held him at arm's length, closely inspecting Caleb's features. "You're thin," he said, "but none the worse for it. No more baby fat, hey? No more baby fat indeed." Releasing Caleb, he swung toward John Stark. Dust blew from his ballooning coat, and Caleb sneezed again. "I hear great things of you, John," Gramp announced. "A hero! Just as we expected! Don't deny it."

Colonel Stark cleared his throat. "I fear you've heard some farfetched tales—"

"No," Caleb cut in quickly. "I was there. The tales are all true. Pa's a real hero."

His father pointed to Caleb. "And here's another. Every man was a hero at the rail fence."

Gramp pursed his lips. "I heard tell. That's why I came. I couldn't stay away. It's been a long, dusty trip. Never have I ridden such a miserable nag as that one I rode today. A pacer, they call him! I have better names for that spawn of Satan! But here I am, ready for the fray!" He struck a pose, as Stark looked at him quizzically.

"I don't just know where we might use you, Captain," Stark said, "but it's good of you to volunteer."

"I'm ready for any post," Gramp assured him. He turned to Caleb. "I know now how you felt when you yearned to join the troops. And I said, 'No, you cannot.' What a mean old man you must think me."

"I bear no hard feelings, Gramp," Caleb assured him. "I hope you hold none toward me."

"Hard feelings!" Gramp exclaimed. "Of course not! The blood that flows in our veins is fighting blood, boy. It can't be denied!"

Caleb felt uncomfortable, remembering how his legs had quivered before the battle. But he decided not to mention that. He spoke to his father. "It seems matters have changed. Do ye mind if I stay here?"

"Well," John Stark said slowly, "you *are* halfway to sixteen. Perhaps we might close one eye."

Caleb grinned. "Thank ye, Pa. Colonel, I mean." He looked reflectively at Gramp. "I'll see what I can do about swearing you into my company as a private. Then I can help ye with such details as digging breastworks."

Gramp puffed out his lips. "A private! Digging breastworks! A man of my age and experience expects better than that!" He paused, seeing a slight smile appear on

Caleb's face. After a moment's pause, an answering smile appeared on Gramp's face. "I see you're trying to discourage me—and that's no doubt a favor." He looked at the Colonel. "Be honest. Is there need for my services?"

"I'd say you'd be of more service at the farm, helping guard the place," John Stark told him honestly, "and keeping your eye on the Snavelys."

Gramp looked dejected. "Maybe so. Someone must serve behind the lines. Properly, I suppose, the task should fall on the old men."

"You've earned the right to your comfort," his son-in-law said quickly. "Let the young bloods carry on the battle."

Captain Page looked at him quizzically. "Young bloods such as yourself, John?"

"Since you put it that way," Stark answered gravely, "I'll admit there are times when my blood does flow a mite sluggish. And my joints do stiffen in the evening damp. In the cold, I ofttime shiver, as with the ague. My eyes grow weary, my limbs heavy. But also I must admit I cannot find it in my heart to follow the advice I so easily give to you. Like an old war horse, I must go where I sniff the powder."

"Don't belittle yourself, John," the Captain said. "Some lads in their twenties seem older in spirit than you."

"Truly, I do feel young in spirit," Stark replied. "It must be I'm sustained by the young cause in which I believe."

"If it affects you thus, what manner of strength it must lend to those still truly young"—Captain Page looked out the window—"such as those lads out there!"

Caleb and his father stepped to the window and stood beside the Captain. Outside, a squad in ragged homespun marched briskly along the dusty road to the beat of "Yankee Doodle."

Caleb felt a tightening in his throat. At long last he was to become part of this bold company. He yearned to be out there, shoulder to shoulder with the marching men.

"We walk a long uphill road," John Stark said softly, "and I fear there is no turning. Pray God we'll reach its end in safety."

Caleb nodded. He was content. From this day on, he and his pa would be marching forward together.

Author's Note

The importance attached to the Battle of Bunker Hill can be gauged by a remark attributed to George Washington. The General had ridden only twenty miles on his journey from Philadelphia to Cambridge, where he was to assume command of his young army, when news of Bunker Hill was brought to him.

His immediate question was, "Did the militia fight?"

When assured that the militia had fought bravely, he said with relief, "Then the liberties of this country are safe."

Through Caleb's involvement in the battle, and in the events that preceded it, we have attempted to dramatize this struggle. Details of the battle itself are believed to be accurate, although our account is limited to action taking place near the rail fence. Officers who participated in the battle are historical figures.

Seizure of the powder at Fort William and Mary also is a historical fact. Caleb was indeed the son of John Stark, and he did run away from his grandfather's house to join his father's forces at Bunker Hill. Captain Demeritt did deliver a portion of the powder taken from Fort William and Mary to Stark's regiment in time to be used at Bunker Hill.

Several fictional characters have been introduced, including Zeb Snavely and Eli Vanderhoff. The time sequence is changed, in order that Caleb personally can help deliver the powder to his father.

There is no account that supports Grandfather Page's trip to John Stark's headquarters, but, knowing the old gentleman as we do, it would have been in character for him to make an appearance there, raring for action.

ABOUT THE AUTHOR

Since his first encounters with English composition in Public School 17, Jersey City, New Jersey, Robert P. Richmond has loved to write. He has held a variety of jobs, including newspaper and magazine editorial positions.

During War II his service in the U.S. Army in the Battle of the Bulge gave him an understanding of the feelings of a young man—like Caleb Stark in this book—undergoing gunfire for the first time. At war's end Mr. Richmond accepted a position with the Veterans' Administration and has been associated with that agency since 1947.

Writing in his spare time, he has reached both adult and juvenile readers of national magazines. POWDER FOR BUNKER HILL is the second book for young people he has written as a result of his continuing study and interest in our country's early history.

The Richmond family lives in Hanover, New Hampshire. Mrs. Richmond—Frances—is librarian in Hanover's elementary school; daughter Carol is at Keene State College in New Hampshire; daughter Marion attends Elmira College in New York State; and a son, Robert, is doing graduate work at the University of Texas.